MAYBE AGAIN

MAYBE AGAIN

MAYBE THIS TIME

JOLIE MOORE

This edition published by

Moore Digital Media Inc
1125 N Fairfax Avenue
Unit #46071
West Hollywood, CA 90046

Cover Designer: Cover Me Darling
eISBN: 978-1-64414-079-6
ISBN: 978-1-64414-080-2

ALSO BY JOLIE MOORE

ONE

"SOY YESENIA MORALES. Por KESP, buenas noches y cuídense."

The camera's red light winked off. At the floor director's signal, Yesenia pulled out her earpiece and allowed her cheek muscles to relax for the first time in a half hour. The rousing Norteña music accompanying the commercial break was in sharp counterpoint to the uncertainty spreading from her chest to her limbs.

This was her last broadcast as temporary weeknight news anchor. Come Monday, Yolanda Salcedo was back from maternity leave. Unless Yesenia did something to kickstart her career, next week she'd be demoted to her regular weekend floating anchor position.

The last time she'd been on the edge of career implosion, she'd saved herself by busting that city-wide cockfighting ring wide open. But lightning didn't strike twice.

Following the beckoning wave from her director, she stood and pulled at the fitted hot pink suit chafing around her breasts and hips. She had to work her way out of local

Spanish language news to someplace where the women anchors weren't gussied up like department store mannequins.

When the red light indicated they were back on the air, Hector's arm slipped around her waist. She did the same, pretending to chat and laugh as they walked off the set.

"And we're out," the floor director called. She and Hector disengaged like the other had cooties. His shellacked hair and peach pancake makeup said one thing to her: dinosaur. It wasn't that she didn't like Hector García. He was a lovely old man from the Tom Brokaw reporting era, respectable, kind, honest. But he didn't get the TMZ tabloid world journalism had become. As far as she could figure, they only kept Hector around to hold on to viewers from her mother's generation.

She stalked to her desk, just another gray pressed wood rectangle in the cubicle farm of the newsroom, waving away the shouted invitations for Friday night drinks.

She sat at her cubicle only long enough to pack her bag and pull off the stilettos she had to wear now that the anchor desk was out. The station brass had replaced it with a Plexiglas stand no wider than a barstool. Gone were the days where she could hide jeans and sheepskin boots under a pressed wood desk. Yesenia stretched her cramped toes and massaged her aching foot after she eased the three inch pumps from one foot, then the other. She held back her groan of relief.

As decreed from up high, her whole body from head to toe was on display. But ratings were up, and that was good for everyone, from station owner on down to a lowly anchor. Viewers were all her bosses cared about these days. And if a little exploitation was what it took to get eyeballs on screens, then so be it.

Yesenia closed her eyes and visualized a weekend spent horizontal. Away from the anchor desk, she planned to fall into bed, and get up only when her mother summoned. Mascara glued her tired eyes together, making them hard to open. Time to get home and get the clown-like goo off. She could only hope the obligatory family dinner this week was Sunday instead of Saturday so she could rest up for whatever her mother and sister planned to throw at her.

Stapled packets of half researched stories littered her desk. One by one she shoved papers into her purse. The last stack was personal and caused her stomach to do a flip-flop. With shaking hands, she cursed her mother, the Catholic Church, and Cameron Becker; three factors that had kept her married but separated, when she should probably be divorced.

A Sale and Purchase agreement for her Ogden Drive apartment stared back at her. The building's landlord was getting out of the rental business, converting the apartments in her building to condominiums. With little down payment, she could own a space of her own. But California's Community Property laws and the mortgage company required that her husband sign off any right to the apartment.

She *needed* the signature of her estranged husband Cam. Nearly two years had come and gone with nothing more passing between them than cursory communication in April when tax season rolled around.

Maybe it was time to rip off the Band-Aid. She pulled her phone from her desk drawer. Fingering the contacts, she hit her husband's picture. But as soon as the phone began dialing, she immediately disconnected the call.

Tomorrow.

Pulling her sneaker laces tight, she prepared for the fourteen-story descent from the station's studios on the top floor of the Sunset Boulevard building.

She did not take elevators.

Her ready excuse was that she always needed to lose a few pounds. And given her mother's penchant for dropping off carb-heavy handmade tortillas and tamales, that part at least was true.

"Yesenia." The news director beckoned before she could make her escape. Nervous energy flooded her veins again.

She trudged the ten feet to Ernesto Barrero's office. Ignoring his gesture to sit, she stood, trying not to shift her weight or show her fear of being fired.

"What are you working on?"

Nothing good, shot through her brain. But she was wise enough not to voice that thought. She sat heavily and made a show of ruffling through the papers in her bag.

"I have a few things coming together," she started, forcing passion into their voice. "That scandal involving the county sheriffs and prisoner abuse. Hispanics were affected in greater numbers than anyone else." Like a dancing minstrel, she continued. "There's also more on the Coliseum corruption scandal. Turns out there are other workers with grievances, mostly Mexican," she said.

"That sounds great if this were *Sixty Minutes*. But we're KESP. Sweeps are right around the corner. Our viewers are looking for sex, drugs, badly behaved rock and rollers." He did an exaggerated shrug. "You know."

"I've got some other irons in the fire," she said, not mentioning those irons were cold, and the fire long banked.

"Yolanda's coming back next week," he said, changing the subject.

Moving to the three to eleven weeknight shifts to cover Yolanda's maternity leave had been exhausting for the last three months. But even when she went back to her regular duties, she'd have more material for her reel. Maybe she could finally make that leap to a local English language station or national broadcasting on Telemundo. Be done with gotcha journalism. Chasing celebrities was one thing. Getting the dirt on reality show stars was a new low. Ernesto was looking at her oddly. Yesenia wondered how long she'd been quiet.

The constant anxiety that had sat in her belly for three months churning through the layers like battery acid, bubbled up. Her throat burned. "What does that mean for me?" Yesenia asked. Maybe she couldn't pull the bandage off the wound of her dead marriage, but work was an altogether different beast. If she was fired, knowing now would be better than later.

"Don't look so down. You did a great job on air. Had a meeting this morning with the higher ups and we're thinking about trying something new."

Even though she didn't want to hang on his every word like a girl waiting to be asked to prom, she couldn't help leaning forward.

"We want to add another woman anchor with Hector, change up the format."

"Me?" God, now she sounded like that prom eager teenager as well, or Sally Field at the Oscars.

"Of course, you." Ernesto said. "I didn't want to tell you before, but the three month stint was mostly an audition." He paused for effect. "You got the part."

Glee replaced fear. A permanent addition to the nightly news would move her career to the next level. If being seen was the name of the game, then daily exposure was the best she could hope for.

"You'd have to wear dresses instead of suits, and keep the high heels." Ernesto said as if exploitation were their every day stock and trade instead of hard news. "You interested?"

"*Sí*, yes," she said without hesitation. She might regret it later, when push-up bras were her currency instead of investigative journalism. But for now, she was willing to stay put at KESP. A steady and hopefully increased paycheck would keep her mother and sister in the country. With a raise she could tuck a little more away for an immigration attorney who could finally get the rest of her family their papers.

Ernesto looked at his watch. "Damn. Past midnight. My wife's going to kill me. Let's talk on the way out."

While snaking through the newsroom, they worked out most of the logistics of her new schedule.

He pushed the elevator button.

For the briefest second she closed her eyes. *Avoid.*
Avoid. Avoid. The words pulsed in her brain like a strobe.
Taking a deep breath to slow her heart rate, she put on her
news anchor smile.

"I'll take the stairs," she said to her boss.

"You're not fat, Yesenia." Ernesto shook his head,
muttering something about L.A. women under his breath.

"Exercise is good. Especially if I'm going to need a
new wardrobe."

She nearly lost the grip on her bag as sweat slicked her
palms. With her free hand, she tried to be as cool as
possible wiping the moisture from her upper lip.

"Let's talk about compensation. It'll be more private
this way." Of course, he wanted to finish the conversation
—in an elevator of all places. That's what normal people
did. Pulling up her big girl panties, she stepped on, careful
not to snag her shoe on the gap between the floor and the
moving box. She needed money and Ernesto had the keys
to the vault.

He punched the button with two arrows facing each
other, and the reflective metal finally started to close them
in. Less than a minute, and the descent to the garage
would be over. In less than a minute, she could be richer.

"Damn. Forgot something. I'll get off. Don't want to
keep you. Good night." Ernesto said, then jabbed at
another button. The doors whooshed open again. "We'll
talk Monday."

Before she could push her way out and get off with
him, the doors slid closed. She was alone. A single jerk
and the box began its descent.

Her heart went from normal to attack range faster

than a Porsche's engine revved from zero to sixty. Post traumatic stress, her first therapist had diagnosed years ago. Sweat trickled under the wire of her bra and down her rib cage. The protein shake she'd had for dinner threatened to come up. Bitter bile made its way to the back of her throat.

She swallowed.

Death was not a reasonable fear. Millions of people suffered panic attacks and recovered every day. She fumbled for her pills then stopped. The alprazolam took at least a half hour to work. An elevator ride had to be less than a minute. Yesenia gritted her teeth against the chatter she could feel prying her jaw apart.

Closing her eyes, she took a deep breath. Held it. Counted to five. Released it. Opening her eyes, Yesenia looked at the red number.

Only five floors to go.

🌱

"YOU WATCHING THE SEXY NEWS?"

"Fuck off," Cameron Becker said to his on again/off again partner.

Jean Rivera was the only woman in the LAPD he could say that to and not be busted down a grade or two. They'd done hundreds of sting operations together when Rivera had been younger and didn't mind dressing up like a hooker. And when he hadn't minded being out on the streets all night, busting johns.

Thank God, they'd both wised up to the fact that street-level busts didn't make a dent in the skin trade about the same time they'd gotten too old for all-nighters.

Rivera came around the break room table to stand next to him. She crossed her arms, mocking his stance. "You look like someone ate your Pop Tart."

Cam uncrossed his arms and tried to do the casual dangle at the side thing he'd seen other men do. Didn't work too well. He crossed them again, tighter this time. Stiff cotton pulled across his biceps. The commercial ended and his ex—his *wife*—came up on screen with Hector something or other joking with Jessie like he was her best friend.

"Ahhh." Rivera drew out the single syllable for a full two seconds, her voice full of distaste. "It's Yesenia."

"She's been anchoring every night," he informed her.

"Finally made the jump from the weekend, huh?" Her voice held no admiration.

"Shh." His heart did the same little skip it did the first time he'd met Jessie. He wondered, not for the first time, if they were ever going to get back together. In the two years apart, the problems that had divided them were less and less important. Jessie gave her signature send off; good night and stay safe. A minute later, her pompadour sporting co-anchor had his hands around her waist, escorting her off set while the credits rolled.

Hector had what Cam wanted, the ability to touch his own wife. Torn between jealousy and attraction, he picked up the remote and muted the set. He hoped Rivera couldn't see the heat he could feel prickling his scalp. Meant his face was probably pinker than it should be.

"Hey! I was watching that," Rivera said.

"No you weren't." He added a bark to his voice to hide his embarrassment. "Go home to your husband."

"What about you?" Rivera turned on him, her brown eyes unrelenting. "Going back to your tiny studio in Noho?"

Because, what? Going home alone was a crime? "Yep."

"Want to get a drink?" she asked, barely masking her yawn.

Cam hated the pity behind the invitation. Bachelors got invited to every dinner, barbecue, and holiday meal in L.A. A party wasn't complete without one. He'd become an accessory—like a Louis Vuitton purse, but not nearly as in demand.

"Early to bed," he deflected.

"Don't you ever get lonely?" she asked.

Women. Why did they always want to pair you up? Occasionally he met a woman at a bar in the nearby arts district. They had a good time. That was it. He wasn't looking to get into a new relationship. The old one still had a hold on him.

"I'm good."

"Why aren't you divorced yet?"

The muscle below Cameron's right eye twitched. Excuses stuck on his dry tongue. For anyone else, he would have dragged out the usual litany; she was Catholic, he had better health insurance. But neither was true.

"Jean?" He lowered his voice to let her know he was serious. She may have been at his wedding. But this was a no-go zone.

Her eyes held his for a long moment. He tried to telegraph that she didn't need to worry. Her eyes were unreadable. Rivera picked up her purse from where she'd rested it on the table. "See you in three."

They'd worked the four-day, ten-hour compressed schedule this week. Unless there was a riot or natural disaster, they'd be back at work after a much needed three-day break.

A flash of red from the TV pulled him back to thoughts of Jessie. It was a commercial for the nightly news. A camera panned up his wife's stocking-clad leg. The voice over urged viewers to tune in again. *Noticias my ass*. There was nothing newsworthy—

"Shit!" Rivera dropped her purse and braced her arms against the door frame.

He heard the rattle of metal and glass before he felt the floor move under his feet. One part of his brain registered that Rivera was safe. For the moment. His training took over. He pulled her under the table, waiting out the shaking.

Ten seconds. Cam ticked off each one in his mind. As quickly as it had begun, it ended. Everything stopped moving as if nothing had happened. The way his heart had accelerated when seeing Jessie minutes ago had nothing on the pounding in his chest, ears, and throat. Blood had expanded too much for his vessels, they were so tight with pressure.

"Let's go!" He moved to his designated command post. Sergeant Sikes barked out orders.

"Rivera, Becker. You have Fountain, Highland, Beverly, Crescent Heights."

Cam committed those perimeter blocks to memory.

The minute the Sergeant was done, he booked it to the supply room, grabbed the first pool keys he could find, and ushered Rivera out the door.

♥

EVERYTHING SHOOK. Yesenia's brand new sneakers slid around like she was on ice. She could barely keep her footing in the tiny elevator. The building rolled back and forth like a marble on a boat, and she went with it. Like Mexico City, the building was going to come apart. Was that the sound of cracking, stucco hitting pavement? Were windows shattering all around her? Minimal sound pierced the sealed box, got past her thundering heart and harsh breath.

Vowing to keep her head, Yesenia spread her legs hip distance apart, brought her head to her knees, wrapped her arms around her legs, and tried to stop the compulsive swallowing of the saliva pooling in her mouth. Uttanasana, the forward fold was to calm the nausea, ease the panic that had bubbled up in her throat for the second time tonight.

Another roll.

A jerk.

Silence.

The carpeted floor welcomed her like a mother's arms. To hell with coping mechanisms. This was life or death. And death was looking more likely with each passing moment.

She was going to die.

In an earthquake.

Like her father.

God was vengeful.

When there was no further movement for seconds, or minutes, or years, she pawed through her bag for her phone. Pressing the home button cast dim light in the elevator. Weren't there emergency lights in these things? How was she in the only elevator in the world where the emergency mechanism failed? She had been right to never trust these contraptions. Especially in Los Angeles, the least disaster-prepared city in the world. After New Orleans.

If she could tell herself that small joke, maybe she wasn't going to die. Not yet.

Taking another deep breath of synthetic carpet, she pushed herself up to sitting and gripped her phone hard. The cool glass of her phone against her palm eased the panic a tiny bit more.

She pressed the small circle lighting up the digital display that had always signified connection with her family, friends, work. A tiny circle spun near the top of the phone, mesmerizing her with its perfection. Lazily, dizzily, the phone sought connection with a cell tower.

It stopped.

No service.

Her mother and sister would be in a panic if she didn't reach them soon. What if they were hurt, their little house crumbled down around them? She couldn't get to them, help them.

The memory of her father's death busted out of the carefully placed closet she'd locked it into. She chanced a look at the ceiling. No pillar bisected it in the way it had separated her from her father in Mexico.

Fear stole her breath. No way was she going to die like her father. With no connection showing on the phone, she dialed anyway. That worked sometimes when she was way out in the field. Some kind of magic would make the phone connect to a tower. If it could work in Sun Valley, a Hollywood elevator shouldn't be a problem.

She punched in the number.

The phone dialed.

Nothing.

Damn.

She couldn't help her family if she couldn't help herself. One deep breath later, she clawed her way up the wood and brass. She pressed her phone on again. A flashlight didn't require a signal. Words had been long rubbed off the emergency button.

That single red plastic protrusion had been her one line of defense against panic. Her very rational therapist had told her that if she were ever overcome, press the button and someone would come to Yesenia's rescue.

She pressed.

Dial tone.

Dialing.

Ringing.

No answer.

Like so much else in L.A., the buttons were for show. Her therapists had said her fear was irrational. But she'd known. She *knew*.

Defeat pulled her back down to the carpeted floor. She shifted from one side to another, trying to keep her stockings from sticking to her thighs. With the movement, a prickle started on her scalp. A bead of water dripped from her nose. She wasn't crying…yet.

The air conditioning must have been off. It would be one of the first non essential systems to go. Suddenly, she couldn't take it a moment longer. The side zip fitted gabardine top was the first to go. Then the skirt. Not giving a crap about runs, she skimmed the stockings from her legs.

The laugh that bubbled from her throat could have been hysteria. She chose to believe it was humor. *If* she was ever rescued, she'd be in a see-through camisole, bra, and thong. Great. Another laugh escaped her lips. She could only hope the paramedic wasn't a fan with a cell phone. The last thing she needed was to see her sweaty, panicked, half-naked self on TMZ. Not that she was that big of a celebrity. But after that other television news reporter started dating the mayor, Spanish language anchors had bigger profiles.

If she was thinking about tabloids and not her imminent death, maybe things were looking up. The elevator jerked, and her phone dropped to the floor, plunging her into darkness.

♥

RIVERA GLANCED HIS WAY, communicating without words. He nodded in agreement. L.A. was never like this, especially on a Friday night. The streets were eerily quiet.

"Staying put for the moment," he said.

"We can only hope." Rivera glanced at the laptop, the map of their sector zoomed in on the screen.

They started on Beverly. There were quite a few valets standing quietly. The busy upscale Friday night crowd had either left before the quake, or were waiting out aftershocks.

He pulled over where a tight knot of citizens stood. "Can you check this out?"

Rivera gave him a strange look. Protocol dictated they step out of the vehicle together.

He held up his phone. "Wanna check on Jessie."

While Rivera, hands on hips, her jacket spread so that her shoulder holster was visible, interrogated the crowd, he dialed his wife.

One ring.

Voicemail.

He didn't leave a message. What could he say to a women deathly afraid of seismic activity? For a moment, he was tempted to call Reina and Dolores, his mother- and sister-in-law, but their neighborhood would be covered by another pair of LAPD officers.

He joined Rivera.

A short man in a blue vest approached him cautiously.

"Can I help you?"

The man shrank back for a minute then continued his approach.

"Piece of brick fell on a customer's car." The man's accent was thick. New arrival.

"Anyone hurt?"

"No. But the rich man's car..."

Cameron looked over to where the man's gaze had drifted. There squatted a Tesla, half a cinderblock lodged in its windshield. The fence from the adjoining property had buckled. Closely planted ficus trees had caught most of the pieces. But this one, not reinforced by rebar, had shattered the glass.

"Who do you work for?"

The man's eyes shifted in his dark, weathered skin. "I won't arrest you if you don't have papers," he assured him.

"Temp service." In halting English, the valet explained the usual morass of hiring undocumented workers. Felipe, as his name tag read, had signed up with a service, who had hired him out to the valet service, which contracted with the restaurant. It was a common arrangement that kept a lot of hands clean of the sordid world of cheap labor.

Cam gave the standard answer. "It's a civil matter." No doubt the car's owner would file a claim with the valet company who would extract money from the worker. Jessie and her sister Dolores had told him these tales hundreds of times. But as he'd been then, he was powerless to fix what was a federal issue.

Back in the car, he drove through increasingly crowded streets and unusually empty restaurants. Looked like bar patrons had called it an early night and hightailed it home, no doubt to be with loved ones.

Lights blazed at a large liquor store. He pulled into the parking lot. Glass and earthquakes didn't mix.

He joined Rivera inside the front door as the small late night staff worked on cleanup efforts. He left her to do a quick tally of the damage and loss.

They hadn't encountered any injuries. Only property damage. So the fact that his heart beat a little fast and his palms were sweating shouldn't have bothered him. The fact that tonight of all nights he couldn't pin down Jessie's whereabouts really shouldn't bother him. But it did.

Cell towers appeared to be overloaded with calls. Considering and dismissing the idea of using an emergency band, he pulled out his cell again. He was on thin ice with the department as it was. Cam didn't want to give them a reason to slap him on the wrist and make another note in his file. It took him a minute to get a signal.

Still nothing from Jessie except voicemail. He fiddled through the contacts on his phone, found and dialed her land line number. She only lived a few minutes from work. He'd seen her on TV at eleven. She could have gotten home before the earthquake.

Rivera joined him. "Maybe ten, twenty thousand in lost wine and liquor," she reported.

"Let's do residential," he said. Cam drove straight to Ogden, grateful Jessie's house was in their sector and he didn't have to make a choice between his wife and following the rules.

"Who lives here?" Rivera asked when they pulled outside the fourplex.

"Jessie isn't answering my calls."

Rivera made herself scarce, talking to the few people outside. He watched her knock on a couple of doors. Probably shut-ins identified by the neighbors.

He pounded on the front door the units shared. Watching the second hand on his watch pulse in time with his heart, he resisted banging on the door again. A man about five foot ten with salt and pepper hair finally answered. Wrapped in a green terry robe, he looked at Cameron warily.

"Can I help you…Officer?"

Lots of people were wary of the LAPD, blacks, gays, the undocumented. There were reasons for that he wasn't proud of as a fellow officer. But he didn't have time to figure out this man's issues or put him at ease.

"You seen Yesenia Morales tonight?"

"The girl who lives in number four?"

"That's her."

"She works nights," the man said. Cam could see that the man thought he'd revealed too much, but didn't have anywhere to backtrack.

"I'm her husband. Just came to check on her."

The man looked even more wary. Rather than push past him and get to Jessie's, he gave more information than he wanted. "We're separated. My partner and I—" He gestured to Rivera who was talking to a few people across the street. "—are doing our sector check."

"I didn't hear her come in," the man said. "But I've been on the phone checking on my parents. They're elderly in North Hills."

"You reach them?"

"Can't get through," he said, pulling his phone from his bathrobe pocket.

"She lost her father in an earthquake. Can't reach her. I'm worried that this may have triggered…something."

The man's eyes went from wary to waver. "Gary," the guy volunteered his first name.

Cameron pulled out his badge. "Can you knock on her door? I'll call Devonshire and see if I can get a report on your parents."

"I have a key. Let me get it and check." He took down

Gary's parents' names and address. Gary shut the door, but Cam didn't mind. He went to the car and got the other division on the horn.

"She's not in there," Gary said, coming out the door, onto the slate steps.

"Your parents are fine," Cam said. "Some stuff from the China cabinet broke, but they have water, gas, and electricity if not phone service."

"Thanks," Gary said. "Hope Yesenia's okay."

"Me too," Cameron said.

Cameron put his phone away for the rest of the drive through the sector.

"We'll drop off the car and head home, Rivera. The next shift's got this covered."

"Thank goodness," Rivera said through her yawn. "I've got three days with my little hellions. Gonna need all the energy I can muster."

On their way back to the station, Rivera looked at him. "What are you going to do once you find her?"

Cam didn't have to ask who they were talking about. "Make sure she's okay."

"That's it?" Rivera's voice was full of doubt.

"That's it. Her father died in an earthquake. I'm not sure all that therapy she had prepared her for this."

"You're not thinking of getting back together, right?"

"No," he said. But he wasn't sure.

"You're just getting back on your feet."

"I know."

"We're putting the finishing touches on the sting. Even with the quake, it'll probably go forward. I think we have all the preliminary evidence we need to do a stake out and make busts."

The red light on the corner of Melrose and La Brea seared his retinas. He didn't need Rivera to remind him of the mess he'd made of his career. How he'd fucked it all up by blabbing department business to Jessie. She'd done what any reporter would do, taken the story and run with it.

Of course, once the cockfighting ring had been exposed on KESP, their evidence had disappeared, and their suspects had blown in the wind. Eight months of late nights and undercover work had come to nothing and so had the possibility of promotion.

"Just because we aren't together doesn't mean I stopped loving her, okay?"

"Got it."

"Natural disasters have a way of bringing up what's important."

"So…?"

Cameron pulled into the lot and tossed the keys to Rivera. "So I'll see you Tuesday night."

♥

THE PANTING she heard was her own breath. How long would the air last? How much air did a human need to survive? Heaviness weighed on her chest like a boulder. Standing would take too much energy, use too much oxygen. Bending, she laid her head against her knees and sipped at the air.

Regret filled the space fear left behind. She should

have worked harder to make her family legal. They had come to America to get the kind of medical help she'd needed. Doctors in L.A. had changed her from an agoraphobic girl into a functioning woman. Her mother was right. Once she'd been granted permanent residency, there had been little pressure to help her mother and sister. Her career had gone sideways too.

In the beginning, Yesenia had thought she'd be a Mexican Christiane Amanpour. The cockfighting ring bust had put her on the map, or so she'd thought. Instead she'd traded her marriage for gotcha journalism. Her greatest aspiration had ratcheted down to Debra Norville.

Her breath calmed. Sitting up again, she felt around until the cool metal and glass of her phone was back in her palm. She pressed the button again and again. One by one, minutes ticked by. Two long hours later, the elevator jerked again. Fluorescent lights flickered on. She shielded her eyes against the glare, looking for an escape.

She was getting out.

Pulling on her skirt as best she could, Yesenia waiting for the box to move. Moving on cables and pulleys didn't scare her any longer. Staying still without air—did. Another jerk. The elevator went up, not down.

It stopped.

Lights out.

It took longer to stop the panting this time. She pressed the phone's home button. The same circle that had been spinning for hours stopped. 4G winked into place.

A signal.

She dialed on autopilot.

One ring.

Connection.

"Cameron Becker."

Sagging in relief, she said what she'd never been able to before. "I need you."

♥

IT WAS near two in the morning when Cam finally got into his Dodge Charger on the station parking lot. He'd been texting with his mom and Ryan off and on while they'd driven their quadrants. His family by blood was safe.

Before he pulled into traffic, he checked his phone one last time. He was surprised to have it ring in his hand. Adrenaline flooded his veins again. Yesenia. His Jessie. His hands shook.

Grabbing the wrist of his phone hand to steady it, he placed the rectangular lifeline to his ear.

He spoke his name into the phone, not sure what in the hell was going to come next. Alive and uninjured was all he wanted.

"I need you," was the last thing he'd expected to hear.

TWO

CAM THREW his personal car in reverse and pushed the gas pedal, hard. The squeal of tires preceded the thud of rubber hitting the concrete bumper. The hazard of not looking behind him.

Running back into the station, he fumbled with the combination lock. Taking a deep breath, he spun the numbers again. With shaking fingers, he made sure the white notch after ten lined up with the tiny red carrot above. Another breath. Eleven notched in. He turned past eleven, then seventeen, then twenty-nine. The lock gave little resistance this time around.

Gym clothes, water, and other supplies joined the flashlight he'd grabbed from his desk drawer. All stuffed into his gym bag, he ran back to his car.

He pressed the phone on. The screen was again a serene picture of a partially cloudy sky. In direct contrast to the light polluted smog above and the feeling of trepidation that lined his gut like lead.

She hadn't called again. Empty streets made his bat-out-of-hell driving—nearly safe. Cameron was at KESP's building on Sunset in ten minutes flat. The small gathering of men in jumpsuits did not inspire confidence. Their air of do nothingness and uncertainty was unsettling. He fought the urge to get LAPD and L.A. Fire Department officers on the scene before he assessed the situation. Now that he walked a career tightrope, he constantly second guessed himself. He hated this. But he didn't want to cost the city tens of thousands of dollars if it was uncalled for.

Striding toward the knot of men, he stood tall. "What's the story?" he asked no one in particular.

Silence greeted his inquiry.

He pulled the gold and silver badge from his pocket. Everyone started talking at once.

He pointed to the guy who looked like he was in charge. "You."

"Officer—"

"Lieutenant Becker to you," he said, not caring about barking out each word.

"Sir, Lieutenant," the suited man started. "Someone is trapped in the elevator." He pulled at a crumpled paper in his hand and read. "Yesenia—"

"Jessie Morales. She's my wife."

That last sentence galvanized the small crowd into action.

Another man emerged from the crowd. From the cell phone in one hand and walkie talkie in another, Cameron gathered he had authority. "Lieutenant, sir, she's been in there a couple of hours. We can't get it restarted."

To hell with this. If they'd been standing around for

hours without resolution, he'd do it. He was trained in search and rescue. "Get me in there."

"In where?" The man's confusion made him wonder if he'd stuttered.

"In the damned elevator." His voice rose above the crowd, silencing the murmurs. "How can I get to the service hatch?"

The man fidgeted with the on/off knob of the walkie talkie, alternately filling the air with static and silence. "The liability—"

"I'll sign whatever damned waiver you need."

The men looked at each other again in a mimic of the circle jerk he'd walked in on. He didn't have time for this.

"She's claustrophobic," he said, trying to press them without revealing the truth behind her fear.

"Do we need a social worker?" the man with the walkie talked asked. His question meandered like he was on a walk in the park and not in the midst of a life and death emergency.

He started to push by them, but decided to use his authority instead of brute strength. Damn the consequences.

Another flash or two of the badge and worry about his expertise at rescue fell by the wayside.

"Do you need—"

"It's a one man job," he threw over his shoulder before he hoisted his black nylon bag over it. By the time he got to the stairs, he dared a glance back. Not one of the men had followed him. But if they'd been men of action, they'd have already rescued his Jessie.

The dim emergency lighting was enough to guide him

up twelve flights of stairs. He went through a fire door toward the elevator shaft.

Bouncing the flashlight beam off all surfaces it could reach, he did a quick assessment. A ten-foot climb down the ladder, and he'd be on the car. With the power shut off while in the shaft, there was little chance of injury. Mini Maglite in his teeth, he made the descent. His gloves made light work of the unused latch. One hard twist and lift was all it took. He was in.

"Jessie?" he called down through the hole.

"Cam? Is that you?" The confident anchor voice was long gone. She sounded as weak as a day old kitten.

"Move to a corner," he ordered as he snapped off the flashlight, tucked it in his pocket. The bag went in first, landing with a heavy thud. Years of pull-ups made lowering himself in easy. "I'm coming in."

As soon as his feet could hit the floor, Jessie sprung from where she'd been and clung to him like her life depended on it. He smoothed back her hair and pressed his lips to the top of her head. Chamomile and aloe filled his nostrils. Cam remembered the scent well. She had always driven out to her mother's neighborhood to buy the Spanish labeled cosmetics. He'd never smelled that combination of earth and flowers on another woman. From scent alone, he'd been able to pick out his wife in a crowd.

For long minutes they stood, or rather Cam stood, leaning against the wall. Her arms and legs gripped him like bands of steel.

"You okay?"

Words tumbled from her in Spanish and English, a

jumbled heap of fear. Turning off the part of his brain striving for comprehension, he aimed for comfort.

"Shh," he whispered again and again until it soothed her like a balm. Finally, the heart that had been pulsing against her chest and his, like a beacon, slowed. Dampness seeped through his clothes. The hand against her back was moist with perspiration. Gently, he set her down, and put the lit flashlight on the floor, giving them faint illumination.

Retrieving the black nylon bag, he zipped the top open. The blanket was out first. He spread it on the floor. Next he pulled a bottle of water and handed it to her. Jessie took large uninhibited swallows. Next he pulled out his gym clothes. "Put these on."

Without the modesty she used to hold dear, Jessie made quick work of shedding what remained of the same half zipped pink suit he'd watched her walk off camera in hours ago. The transformation between this Jessie and the one he married distracted him from thoughts of rescue. He closed his eyes, keeping the reality of her at bay.

She'd been that stereotypical Catholic school girl when he'd met her, short skirts and modesty. The contradiction had turned him on and driven him mad. Many months of sex in the dark and robes during the day had nearly driven him around the bend. He'd coaxed her out of her clothes slowly, all the while letting her know she was the most beautiful women he'd ever known.

Jessie had shed some of the guilt, especially after they married, but she'd held onto her other ideals, which was why they were still legally married.

With the buzz of the zipper and the whoosh of satin,

he couldn't resist opening his eyes. She pulled on his LAPD t-shirt. It dwarfed her, falling to her knees. Cam closed his eyes trying to forget the other times she'd worn his clothes. But it didn't help. The backs of his eyelids merely served as a screen. Memories of long weekends in bed flickered away. He'd loved to put his shirts on her then take them off slowly.

"Cam?" his name was a question. Snapping open his eyes, he fished out shorts. *"Gracias,"* she said softly as she rolled the top down on his shorts to keep them from falling from her hips.

"It's nothing," he said translating his response from Spanish to English in his head.

*"Cuando...*when, how long—" There was no need for her to finish. Her breaths were growing rapid again. Her hands fidgeted with her rings, her watch, his clothes. She wanted, no, needed out of there, bad.

For once, Cam played fast and loose with the truth. "An hour, maybe two," he finally answered. He'd heard the men out there talking about needing twenty four hours to get the elevator started, but that information would be too much for Jessie.

After she'd explained what had happened during that devastating Mexico City quake, he'd never taken her fear of elevators for granted. Fortunately, in a low-slung city like Los Angeles, she hardly ever had to walk up more than three or four flights of stairs. And she'd mastered the fourteen it took to get to her newsroom years ago.

He'd climbed thousands of steps in the city. Even when she'd needed to get her immigration papers straightened out, he'd trekked the ten flights necessary to avoid her anxiety attacks. Plus, he was a guy and the view was great. When she'd gone first, a peek under her skirt had been well worth the burning quads.

"How is it out there?" she asked, her breathing returning to normal again.

"Five point one. Epicenter was Baldwin Hills."

"Damage?" she asked. Her voice almost sounded normal. Jessie was back in anchor mode.

He shook his head. Now would not be the time to mention he'd met her neighbor and her place had seemed okay from the outside. He stuck with a generic answer. "Nothing much on the ride through."

The elevator ascended an inch, two, then stopped. Her face went from normal to panic in the flashlight's beam.

"Why am I stuck?" The question rushed from her with a squeak. She turned away, looking embarrassed.

"Place was built in the late sixties. Power went out with the quake. The backup generators are keeping the station on the air. Elevators weren't the first priority." He shrugged. "Taking some time to reset the system."

Pulling out a second bottle of water, he took a swig and handed it to her. She pushed it away, instead bending at the waist, curling her hand around her knees. She mumbled what sounded like a prayer in Spanish. Her dark hair swept back and forth across the carpeted floor as she swayed a little.

He needed to keep her talking, keep her calm. "How'd you end up here?" he asked. She was the dead last person he'd expect stuck in an elevator during an earthquake.

"Boss wanted to talk about me filling in permanently on the weeknight anchor desk." The answer filtered up through her hair. Her voice sounded near normal, but she hadn't yet abandoned the yoga pose. Keep her talking, he told himself. It's what he'd do with any other hostage or victim.

"Not exactly a desk," he said, not trying to hide the irritation from his voice. Wasn't the best thing he could have said. He wanted to keep things low-key, not start a fight.

She sighed. Her arms came out like airplane wings. Jessie soared to standing, her hands coming together in some yoga pose, descending between her breasts. "Cam, that's what sells now. Channel thirteen did it first. The rest followed. No biggie."

He bit his tongue. They'd already fought about the exploitive nature of her job and dozens of other little things about Ernesto and KESP. Being separated meant they didn't have to do that anymore.

The air from the open hatch had cooled the elevator, but Jessie still looked a little worse for wear. He dug around in the duffle bag again and extracted some anti bacterial wipes.

"Your makeup—"

Jessie swiped a single finger across her cheek smearing black and pink.

He reached toward her. "Here. Let me." Carefully he wiped sweat and makeup that had streaked her face. "Better?"

She nodded, not opening the eyes she'd closed when he'd swabbed her lids. Despite indulging in his not so secret vice of watching her every day on the news, he hadn't been this close to her in years. Pushing papers across the library's reading room tables to sign tax forms didn't count.

He took his own deep breath, calming his heart. The attraction was there as strong as ever. Jessie's wavy dark hair wasn't girlishly long, like when they'd met, but a blunt shoulder length instead.

They were so far away in time and place from the young beat cop who'd arrested Raul and picked up Dolores in a mid-city sweep.

When Jessie's sister had finally given up her family's phone number, he'd been relieved. Raul had gone downtown to central booking, and the defiant teen had sat, arms crossed and mad in the Wilshire station for three long hours.

He'd handed Dolores off to her sister, but made a note of their contact details. Dolores and Reina hadn't been too thrilled when he'd stopped by to check on the family. But Jessie had accepted his invitation to dinner. They'd had so much in common, lively mothers, tragically dead fathers, ambition, attraction.

He'd wanted to marry her right away. But she'd put him off for nearly a year, thinking he'd walk away when he found out she and her family were undocumented. Of course he hadn't. How could he? They'd worked together diligently to get Jessie's green card, and she'd stopped working off the books jobs and started working for KESP.

He shook his head. A trip down memory lane wasn't a good idea. He knew how the story played out. Where they'd ended up, despite their promising start.

"How's your mom?" he asked, then regretted it immediately. Reina Prado had been one of the splinters in their marriage. Her constant nagging about Jessie's responsibilities to her family had kept his wife on edge. It was one the reasons she was always trying to work harder, push farther. To try to make the American dream come true for her mother and sister.

Jessie relieved his anguish over dropping that bomb by keeping things light. Her smile warmed him from across the car. "Cooking as always."

Cam looked at her again. It hurt a little less each time. Memories didn't knock him for a loop with this third glance. Maybe they should see each other more often. That way the shock of attraction and the pang of regret wouldn't be so sharp. "Big *Cinco de Mayo* party?" he managed.

"Always," she said. For the next hour he kept her talking about her sister, her mom, the entire South L.A. neighborhood he used to visit weekly. With each sentence, her breathing eased. Her voice grew steadier.

He snapped off the flashlight when it flickered. "Forgot to check the batteries. We need to conserve energy."

Her watch glowed faintly in the darkness, casting her chin in fluorescent green. "I thought you said an hour." The voice was up an octave.

An hour had been ambitious. Cursing himself for not thinking to swap out the batteries, he spoke rapidly, trying to take the edge off her fears. "The elevator may work before the lights are on everywhere. Don't want to navigate in the dark."

"Are you telling the truth, Cameron?"

He crossed his fingers behind his back, forgiving

himself the little white lie he was about to tell. "Yep. I talked to the building staff before they let me up here. You don't think they'd want two people stuck in an elevator for days, do you?" Silence stretched between them. He resisted the urge to pull her into his arms. But solace wasn't what she sought from him anymore.

The big Mexico City earthquake was the line in the sand. Before that, her family had lived happily in Mexico. After that, Reina had sold off everything the family'd had to hire a *coyote* and bring them here. It was the middle of the story that he'd never dared to ask.

But they'd already lost their marriage. There wasn't much else to lose. So he blurted out the thing he'd always wondered.

"How did your dad die?" The minute the words left his mouth, he silently cursed himself a thousand times a fool. His curiosity of a moment ago was nothing but selfish. No one but a complete and total ass poked a sharp stick at the single biggest gaping wound in her heart. Before Cam could take it back, pretend it had never happened, she answered.

"Trying to save me." Her words were so quiet it took him a good minute to get them through his brain. All at once, those four words hit him like a ton of bricks.

"Ah, fuck," he said softly. The sharp stick he'd poked at her, jabbed him in the heart. His own father had met his bitter end in an accident. Nearly twenty years later, the injustice of his dad's death pulsed behind his eyeballs.

Jessie's breath hitched. He groped for her hand in the near dark. Finding it, he intertwined their fingers. He asked the question he'd never had the guts to ask because he'd never wanted to answer it himself. "What happened?" But talking would be better than crying.

"Fue jueves." The whisper of sound was her shaking her head. She'd always done that when starting in the "wrong" language. Switching to English, she said. "It was Thursday. My dad was taking me to school because Mama was home with Dolores, who was sick with a bad cough."

When she paused, he gripped her fingers harder, and with both of his, pulled her hand into his lap.

"Did Reina usually take you to school?"

"Of course. I was only seven. Mama, Dori and me did it every day. I was so happy to have time alone with Papa."

"But you didn't get to school?"

"Only the elevator. We were going down when everything started to shake. *El terremoto*, it was the longest two minutes of my life. Just like tonight, the elevator fell a few stories. But that time, my dad banged his head pretty hard. I saw blood coming from the side, but he said he was okay."

Cameron could hear the hope of that little girl come through Jessie's voice.

"But I thought he was going to be fine," she continued. "I'd seen my cousins bleed all over the place from stupid accidents."

He squeezed her hand. He knew all about that. Having a brother only two years younger, he and Ryan had their share of fights that ended with broken furniture and trips to the emergency room for stitches.

"How long were you in there?"

"Hours. He told me stories about growing up in

Mexico City. It was almost fun, you know. I had my dad to myself. And I was okay missing the spelling test."

A hiccoughed laugh escaped her throat. He squeezed her hand again, trying to keep the hysteria he could hear around the edges of her voice at bay.

"My biggest worry that day was a ruler across the knuckles from Sister Maria Avalos." Her voice was rueful. The adult Jessie marveling at the inconsequential worry.

"What then?"

"The building shook again. This time a pillar came through the elevator separating us. I could no longer see him. To keep me from panicking, he was still telling stories, but his voice got softer and quieter until he stopped speaking."

"I'm sorry," Cam said.

Jessie continued as if she hadn't heard him. She spoke like she was in a dream, watching it, not reliving it. "I thought he'd fallen asleep. Until I didn't hear any breath any more. I was seven, but I wasn't stupid. In my heart, I knew."

"How'd you get out?" Cameron asked.

"*Mi tío*. He was the one that found me. Took me to Mama." Jessie's voice went flat. "I had to be the one to tell her Papa was dead."

Before he thought better of it, Cameron pulled her into his arms. They weren't man and wife in the way they used to be, but he wanted to give her comfort. Ease her suffering. Jessie shook like a ficus leaf in the Santa Ana winds. His shoulder grew wet with tears.

"Shh. I didn't know. I'm sorry." He'd always thought it was something like that. But her family almost never talked about the Mexico quake. Even on *Día de los Muertos*, when they honored her father's death, they only talked about his life. The only good thing to come of the quake is that it had been the catalyst that had brought the family to the United States. Bringing Jessie to Los Angeles and him.

Pulling her tighter against him, he let her cry for the little girl who had lost her daddy. Where he'd harbored only a hard nugget of anger of his father's accident at Strohmeyer's, Jessie had kept in sadness.

He added not talking to his wife, really talking to her, to his long list of life regrets. He'd mistaken sex for intimacy. If he'd known she'd witnessed death firsthand... he'd have.... Cam didn't know what he'd have done different. Probably a whole lot of things.

The lights flickered on, holding steady this time. Jessie jumped away from him like he harbored a communicative disease.

A disembodied voice filled the cabin. "We're taking the car to the lobby."

That was their only warning. His wife stood, grabbed the brass rail. She held on like it was a death-defying rollercoaster ride while they descended the ten floors to the bottom. He was as useless to her as a sixth finger. The minute the doors eased apart, he reached for her, but grasped nothing but air.

Paramedics and a camera crew swarmed the elevator. He watched his wife's profile transform from scared to self-assured with a single swallow. Jessie turned on the charm when the microphone neared her face.

He swatted away an EMT like a fly. Slowly, he folded

the blanket, putting it and the empty water bottles into his duffle. No one approached him as he walked from the elevator to the corner of the lobby.

Jessie did a dramatic rendition of her entrapment in Spanish, then English. It would play on all the local news stations, he was sure. Angelenos were glued to their televisions when it came to three things: car chases, weather, and earthquakes.

He stood at a distance, watching it all play out. The look he gave the reporters who dared turn his way stopped them in their tracks. He'd watched his career advancement stall out over being the subject of a news story. That was never going to happen again.

When the hot, white camera lights switched off, the paramedics made one last attempt to help his wife.

"I'm fine, really," Jessie assured them. Soon everyone was gone, the news crew out the front door, and the techs down to the electrical panels that were the elevator's brain. It was dawn. Only the two of them remained.

She must have hidden them for the cameras, but suddenly fine tremors radiated through her body. He could see Jessie working to keep it all together.

"I'll take you home," he said, his tone brooking no argument. She followed him to his car. He pulled the police placard from under the windshield wiper and drove her home.

♥

GRIPPING the door handle like a vice was the only way Jessie could think of to control the emotions swirling inside. Fear, relief, regret, and love pulled her heart in four different directions.

It took a few blocks for her to get out of her own head and realize Cameron hadn't asked for directions. "Don't you need the address?" she asked as he pointed his car unerringly toward her house.

"No," was his swift reply. She couldn't decide whether to be angry or grateful. She should have known he'd have her address. Jessie wouldn't have been at all surprised to learn that he had a squad car swing by her house every now and then.

"Once mine, always mine," he'd said on their wedding day. She'd chalked it up to macho crap back then. But now that he'd come to her rescue without hesitation or bitterness, she was sure he'd meant it.

At her building on Ogden, he pulled open the passenger door and took her bag.

Despite her damsel in distress routine from a few hours ago, she still had some pride. "You don't need to—"

"Yes I do," Cam said in the voice he probably used to cow criminals. Waiting a moment for her go first, he walked her to the door. How he found the keys so swiftly in the jumble of her bag, she didn't have a clue. But he pushed open the door to the ground floor apartment entrance and escorted Yesenia in.

What did a person owe to her ex-husband who'd saved her from being trapped in an elevator during the biggest quake Los Angeles had seen in a decade? She'd spent much of her childhood mimicking the manners of successful Americans, but there was no model for this.

"You want some coffee?" she threw out. He ignored her, instead taking the stairs two at a time.

A minute later he called down the stairs, "Jessie, you need to see this." She tried not to bristle. He was the only person she'd allowed to use her *gringa* nickname after high school had ended and Mexican pride had kicked back in.

Taking a deep breath, she made her way up the steps, gripping the iron railing tight. She didn't want to fall if there was an aftershock. Testing the bolts with a little shake, the metal held firm.

When she found him, he was prowling around the second story of her townhouse apartment.

"See this crack," he said, pointing to a new diagonal line in the plaster of the guest bedroom. "Have your landlord check on this."

Her eyes followed the hairline crack. If all went according to plan, she'd be her own landlord soon and this kind of thing would be her problem. Maybe she could make that coffee and invite Cam to sit at the table. She could ask him to sign the papers. Fingers crossed, in a few weeks she'd be the owner of this place, cracks and all.

He was in the guest bedroom when she looked around, ready to execute her plan. "Someone sleeping here?" He pointed to the mussed bed. "Your sister back?"

"*Mí hermana,*" Yesenia started. Then stopped. She wasn't going to defend her family or her actions. And she wasn't going to give him the papers now. Maybe later, when he called to check up on her. Because of course he would call. They hadn't broken up because he didn't care for her. "I think you should go," she said, trying to sound firmer than the jelly jiggling inside where her resolve should have been.

"Not done up here." He strode to her bedroom. She followed in his wake.

"Cam, is this really necessary?" she asked. Adrenaline that had propelled Yesenia for so many hours had worn off the minute she'd stepped into her own home. She was all done pretending she was okay. To turn off her phone, and curl up in bed for a day or two or ten was all she wanted. She needed time to pull her thoughts together. Maybe get an emergency appointment with her old therapist.

As if reading her thoughts, Cam pulled down the bedroom window shades. He slipped the heavy curtains across their rods. "You should sleep."

Her arms crossed in front, ready to pull Cam's shirt over her head. But she hesitated. She hadn't undressed in front of him in years. Except for a few hours ago, she remembered. She hadn't been embarrassed when she thought she was going to die. Suddenly she was as nervous as that third or fourth date when Cam had taken her back to his apartment.

If eyes were windows to the soul, she needed to close hers fast. As if she didn't give a damn about her husband in the room, she pulled off his shirt and wiggled out of his shorts. She extended her hand to return the borrowed clothes.

Cam came closer. It was like the elevator all over again. Suddenly she couldn't pull enough oxygen into her lungs. But it wasn't panic causing shortness of breath this time. It was another thing entirely.

Dolores had always asked what she saw in this shorn stocky white guy with Law and Order as his middle names. Not the law. Definitely not the order. Not the hair or his wordlessness.

It was this.

He looked at her like no other man had. Cameron saw *her*. Not an undocumented immigrant. Not someone's potential housekeeper or nanny. Not some nameless, faceless Mexican woman in Los Angeles, but her. It was something not a single other man had ever tried or accomplished.

He took the clothes and tossed them toward the closet. He came even closer. Yesenia hadn't been married to him for all these years without learning a thing or two about Cameron Becker. What she knew now without a shadow of a doubt is that he wanted her in this bed. That he wanted to make her his like he'd done so many times before. His eyes held hers with single-minded determination. He was going to kiss her.

His big fingers pushed through the hair at her nape and held her jaw steady. She pulled in breath, gathering the strength to flee, to protest—to say yes. But nothing came from her mouth except breath. In an instant, his lips were on hers, making short work of any resistance Yesenia could have mustered. She cursed God above when his tongue met hers. This man wasn't going anywhere for a while.

The kiss turned from soothing to soulful in a heartbeat. Yesenia's hands went around his waist, pulling him closer. Regret over their time apart shook her to the core. All her indignation, anger, and strongly held beliefs didn't grip her as tightly as Cam.

The soft material of his shirt slid upward in her grasp, exposing the toned muscles of his abdomen. He still worked out. The familiar arrow of blond tickled her palm as she followed it up to where the patch of hair fanned out on his chest. Locating his small nipple, she zeroed in with her thumb.

His swift intake of breath unfused their mouths. "Jessie, fuck," he groaned.

"*Yo sé*," she said, pulling the dark blue cotton over his head. He didn't pretend to misunderstand. In the morning light, escaping from the space between the curtains, he was even larger than she remembered. His arms were all muscle, as big and thick as the branches on the decades-old ficus outside her bedroom window.

Big hands. Yesenia had always loved Cam's. Blunt-tipped fingers whispering against her skin, and flat palms skimming her sides had always made her feel small and delicate, though she was anything but. Those hands she'd missed shoved up her camisole and bra.

The cool air on her exposed breasts was immediately replaced by Cam's heat. First from his chest as he moved inexorably closer and kissed her again. Then from the hands he snaked up her ribcage. Each measured the weight of her breasts, as if merging reality with memory.

"*Por favor, tócame.*" Please, touch me.

Like Astaire and Rogers reunited, the old mating dance steps came right back. Cam marched her to the queen-sized bed she'd bought on an indulgent whim. He sat and pulled her with him until they were lying facing each other. Like a starving man, he devoured her mouth. Each thumb fondled a nipple to hardness. She nearly came from that simple touch alone. It had been so damned long.

For long minutes he rubbed her nipples, dipping down to first kiss, then suck. He didn't make an attempt to finish disrobing her. He left her camisole where it rested across her breasts. Her underwear remained firmly in place. Full nudity would have been too much for both of them.

It had always been like this between them. This explosion, like two atoms colliding. When she'd been angry or he'd been silent, the desire between them had never waned. Before she'd finally gotten the courage to walk out, she'd had to cut him off like a dieter giving up sweets. One day at a time she'd weaned herself enough until leaving hadn't stopped her breath.

Yesenia pushed a hand against his chest. He didn't move. But he stopped touching her for a moment. Long enough to gather what wits she hadn't dropped on the floor the moment he'd stepped into her bedroom.

He looked at her long and hard. Eyes the color of the ocean, and nearly as turbulent as the Pacific, met hers. Hair she'd never seen longer than the inch it was now, stood on end. Cam must have racked his hand through it a thousand times over the last six or seven hours.

"Cameron. I don't know," she whispered in his ear, making one last fight to save her hard won independence. But in that single moment of hesitation, the tremors returned. She shook harder than the ground had a few hours earlier when the peril had been real.

"Say yes to this, Jessie."

She closed her eyes for a long moment. His breath fluttered her lashes. Opening them again, she nodded. Decision made, desire replaced fear.

His eyes didn't leave hers. He reached down and pulled the thong between her legs aside. Finally releasing her from his gaze, he broke eye contact to concentrate on what he was doing. Yesenia couldn't look. Looking would be admitting what was happening. What she'd promised herself would never happen again.

¡Dios mío! Yesenia didn't need to see. She swallowed her gasp of pleasure. In and out went his finger. His gaze found hers again. But his stare was so intense, she had to close her eyes. Turned out that wasn't any better. With one sense eliminated, all the rest went on overload. Cam's thumb joined his other finger, this time on her clit. Yesenia gave herself over to the inevitability of the mounting pleasure and release.

"Turn over," he said. Following orders, she turned laying on her other side, her back to his front. Fabric against fabric was the sound of him shucking his pants, and whatever else he had on. Back and forth, he rubbed his erection against her.

Fingers pressed into her thigh. "Let me…"

Following his lead, she lifted her leg. The grip on her thigh tightened. Then Cameron was there thrusting inside her. Doubly shocked, she lost her breath. They'd never done it in any position other than missionary. During all those years, she'd worn her inhibitions like a cloak in bed. But this laid her desires bare before him. Yesenia squeezed her eyes shut. It was so good. She'd never been so filled.

First slowly, then faster and harder, he moved in and out with delicious friction until she heard him shout as if his orgasm had been wrenched from his closed fist. He'd never come without a fight. Always a fight between the tightly wound man and his baser instincts.

What she'd shut out from her mind, her body hadn't forgotten. With the help of his deft fingers, she hit a second crest.

"Why did we get separated?" Cam whispered in her ear right before she fell into the welcome oblivion of sleep. She only answered in her head. Because their sex life had never been the problem. Everything else had.

THREE

YESENIA KNEW an opportunity when she saw one. It's one of the things that made her a good investigative journalist. Leaving Cameron dead to the world, she finally finished the coffee she'd offered hours ago. She was well into the second cup, when Cam shuffled into the kitchen.

At least he'd put on his briefs. He used to walk around their house as naked as the day he was born. Memories of their past tangled with what had happened a few hours earlier. She turned from him, opened the tap and ran her wrists under the cool water. When she'd gotten herself under control she faced him again.

"Coffee?" he asked, gesturing toward the chrome pot on the counter. In the morning he'd always served himself. Then she remembered. Of course, he'd never been here before. She pulled a mug from the cabinet with a handle big enough to accommodate his hands.

"Sit," she said, directing him to a seat at the kitchen table. He pulled the chair out, but not before picking up the pile of papers on the table as if to set them aside. "Don't move those. I need you to sign something."

If he hadn't been so tired, his face, grooved with sleeplessness and worry, would have worn a perplexed look. She turned and made him coffee exactly how he'd always liked it. White, no sugar. She placed it on the table in front of him. He took a cautious sip.

"It's not poisoned."

The joke fell flat. She pulled some so-called breakfast cookies from a top cabinet. He used to love the lemon vanilla treats. Out of habit, she still bought them. She put two on a plate and slid it next to his mug.

"What is this?" he asked, gesturing to the papers she'd lifted from her bag a little earlier. Putting them out on the table had been like lifting a yoke of responsibility from her shoulders. She didn't need to carry the mantle of the Catholic Church any longer. Other Catholics got divorced. The Vatican had weddings of people who co-habitated before marriage and even had kids out of wedlock. Her divorce would be a small sin in comparison.

"The owner of this building wants to sell," she started, easing into the bigger issues.

"Okay."

"He's converting to condos." She paused for a long moment, trying to read him. He sipped, but wasn't giving anything away. "Rather than pay the relocation fee, he's offered to sell me the unit below market."

"What's the catch?"

"For me, none. I would finally get to own something of my own."

"What about the house on Alsace? You remember the

one we bought for your family instead of buying one for ourselves." There was no sarcasm in his tone, but it was a blow to the solar plexus nonetheless. The cold tile of the counter dug into her back as she leaned heavily. Could they not do this without an argument? Without him digging up the past.

Yesenia moved away from the counter and sat across from him. In only a few words, he'd pricked her enthusiasm like a balloon. She wouldn't argue. There would be no yelling. She took one deep breath. Two. It wasn't enough. She took one more. Then went for the same tone she'd use to throw it to the traffic reporter.

"That house is for Mama and Delores. I lived there before we got married, and after we separated. Living here had been…" She fought for words that didn't implicate her, make her feel guilty, show her for the selfish American she'd become. "I like being close to work," she said. Avoiding traffic was always an acceptable justification.

He leaned forward, stretching across the table, sweeping her hair behind her ear. All the fight went out of her. Even Cam looked like he wasn't up for the battle. "You don't have to make excuses for me. What do you need me to sign?"

Thank God in heaven above. This was going to be easier than she'd thought. She pushed the papers back toward him. "I need you to sign this." She put her finger on a signature line highlighted with fluorescent ink. Flipped to another page, showed him the other.

Cameron had never been the kind of man to sign now, read later. Taking long pulls of coffee, he read.

Without him having to ask, she refilled his cup, stirred in cream.

He ate the cookies in two bites. His eyes were intense when he looked up at her. "You want me to sign away any right to this place?"

Gathering her thoughts in English, she spoke quickly. "I don't want you to be on the hook for the loan. You already are for Mama's house. The bank won't lend me money if you don't sign away something they call dower and a...quitclaim deed." She heard herself mispronounce that word, quitclaim. She'd been practicing it and still she'd gotten in wrong. She was ready to shuffle through the papers and show him what she meant, when a meaty hand came down on all of them, stopping her fidgeting.

"We're married." He said it with such finality she wondered if he'd been in the same marriage as she.

"We're separated, Cam." He'd been the one who'd mentioned divorce. She'd been the one hamstrung by the Catholic Church. Well, no more of that. Maybe she'd never take communion again, but the world would continue to spin. Hell was a long way away.

"So this is it, isn't it?"

Yesenia had envisioned this discussion in a coffee shop, or at the front desk of the Hollywood division, maybe even in the little brick public library where they'd met to sign tax returns last year. Somewhere he didn't dare show the full force of his anger.

"Before...before last night I was going to call you."

Cam sat up straight and crossed his arms. Five years ago, she would have backed down. Even three years ago, she would have let his unblinking cop stare keep her silent. No longer. "Say it, Jessie," he dared her.

She matched his height and posture, leaning forward. "I was planning to ask you for a divorce."

"You still want that divorce?" he asked, like one early morning session of mind-blowing sex would change her mind. But the shaking of the ground had hardened her resolve. Life could end any minute. She wanted to start living hers.

Setting aside the eternal damnation of her soul, she nodded. "Yes."

Cameron's utter quiet unnerved her. But she fought to use the best reporter tool she'd ever learned: silence. If she wasn't compelled to fill it, the other person would have to. She was ready to refute anything he had to say. It had taken her weeks to get armed, but her arsenal was ready.

His mouth opened then shut when the shrieking of the phone pierced that silence. There were only two people with her land line phone number. One of them was sitting right at the table, no phone in sight.

"Your mother?" Cameron raised an eyebrow.

Suddenly animated, Yesenia pushed away from the table and grabbed for the receiver. The phone's shriek merged with her mother's wail when she picked up the old-fashioned receiver from the kitchen wall.

"*¿Por que no llamaste?*" her mother whined into the phone. In a single sentence Yesenia was transformed from self-assured adult to a little girl.

She wasn't going to tell Mama the real reason she hadn't called. That she'd forgotten everything the moment

Cam had kissed her. Making her excuses she said, "*Lo siento*. It was near dawn, Mama."

"I had to hear about my own daughter's welfare from the TV!" It would take a year of apologies for her mother to forgive her the sin of not calling after an earthquake. Mama's fear of losing her daughter in the same way she lost her husband had probably turned her hair white.

"I'm sorry, Mama," she said uselessly.

"After what happened to your father, you could have called anytime. Day or night. It wasn't like I was sleeping anyway. You could have *died*! Died!"

Like her father had died. Guilt took away her breath. With a few words, she and Mama were at the crux of their disconnection. Yesenia hadn't saved her father's life. Her mother had never forgiven her. She'd never forgiven herself. So she gave her mother the only thing she could sacrifice, herself.

"I'll be over in an hour, Mama."

"Thank the Lord above. I need to see you in person to make sure you're okay."

She hung the phone in her cradle and turned back to her husband.

"I really appreciated your help yesterday—"

"Why don't you take a shower? Get dressed."

"About the papers."

"We'll discuss it later."

"I'll call you."

"I'm not going anywhere."

"I'm going to Mama's."

"You need a ride."

"I can drive myself. I learned when I was sixteen. I'm okay now, Cameron. I was a little shaken up, but—"

"With what car?" he challenged.

She ran to the living room window, scanning up and down the street. No Jeep. Had it been towed? What in the hell? Cameron's approach had been nearly silent. "It's at the TV station," he said from directly behind her. "I drove you home this morning."

Right. "Can you take me to my car?"

"You're not going back into that underground garage right now. Not until an engineer checks out the structural impact of the quake."

"So?"

"You need to get ready so you're not late for lunch."

She wanted to finish their discussion on the condo, the divorce, the end of their relationship, but her mother waited. If she wasn't at Mama's house in an hour, the phone would ring again and Mama wouldn't be so forgiving the second time around.

She pulled clothes out of her closet and took them to the bathroom, locking the door behind her.

Yesenia was adjusting her skirt, making sure the hem fell below her knees, when Cameron called up that he was ready to go when she was. Buttoning her cardigan more than halfway, she descended the stairs, her grip on the iron railing a little looser this time.

Dressed, he stood at the bottom of the steps. He looked down at her stockinged feet.

"Your shoes."

Yesenia looked longingly at the shearling boots propped haphazardly near the door before trudging upstairs for hard-soled flats that would save her some maternal criticism. Creature comfort and mothers did not go together. Back downstairs, she transferred her makeup, keys and wallet from the designer purse to an inconspicuous canvas tote.

Cam was in either the living room or kitchen, but the front door stood open. She locked her door and joined her husband. A neighbor carrying groceries gave wide berth. He'd taken up a post on the front steps. His arms were crossed, biceps flexed. Mirrored aviators shielded his eyes. She rolled her own. Why did he have to do "cop" twenty-four hours a day?

Yesenia stumbled when her heart gave a knock and her stomach fluttered. She tried to cover her reaction to him by pretending to drop her keys. Before she could take another step, Cam's hand gripped her arm, steadying her. In less than a second, he'd scooped up her keys and dropped them in her purse.

He was saving her, again. She hadn't always needed the hero. But she'd always wanted the man. She'd had too much of the former and not enough of the latter.

Pushing the thoughts of their failed marriage out of her head, Yesenia let him walk her to his car. Again, no directions were necessary. He'd gone to Mama's house nearly weekly for years. Turning her gaze away from Cam, she watched the scenery change from mature trees and upscale cars she'd gotten used to in her new neighborhood to the barren landscape of south Los Angeles.

The absence of foliage, the presence of discarded couches hadn't registered on her radar as marks of poverty until years after she'd been in the country. It had taken a long time to understand why movie stars didn't live in her South L.A. neighborhood.

At first, as a naïve child, she'd only seen the similarities. They had green lawns, blue skies, and perfect weather, just like Beverly Hills. She'd traveled the long boulevards from school to therapy on the bus, unable to see the difference between here and there. But by high school, she got it.

Those other neighborhoods north of Wilshire weren't bombarded with constant sirens, the relentless *whomp-whomp* of helicopter rotors, or the *pop-pop-pop* of gun fire that sounded nothing like the movies. Drive-by shootings and gang warfare completely bypassed white L.A.

"She got bars?" he asked as they pulled up to the single story, gray stuccoed bungalow on Alsace, well south of Wilshire Boulevard. Her mother's house nearly kissed the Santa Monica freeway.

"After some neighborhood break-ins," Yesenia said, pushing the passenger door open before he could.

But he was at the door before she could step a foot on the curb. "Do they have safety latches?" he asked while taking her arm and guiding her out.

"I don't know, Cam."

"But if there's a fire —"

"I can't afford to retrofit them right now," she said with finality.

"You're still supporting them?"

From the moment she could work under the table, she'd supported her mom and sister. "The mortgage gets paid. Your credit is intact." She hoped that was enough for him. She didn't want to talk about her family. About the strain of paying mortgage, rent, a car note. About the guilt she felt because she resented having to do it all. She deflected in the best way she knew how. "Do you still send your mom money?"

Bridget Becker was infamous for always needing something. But instead of asking like Mama, she'd always manipulated her boys into ponying up.

"That's different," he said, crossing his big arms again. Yeah, sure. Cam and his brother Ryan supported *their* mother because it was the *right* thing to do. Somehow supplementing the household income of her own family was *enabling*.

Bridget Becker had always treated Yesenia like she'd trapped her oldest son into a green card marriage. But she'd grown up with her own single mom and manners, so she'd always treated his mom with kid gloves. No matter, her sharp tongue always got in a lash.

"Yeah, it's always *different* with her."

"She always worked an honest job."

"Stop." Yesenia turned toward the door. She'd hated watching her neighbors argue on the front lawn. She wasn't about to take the bait he'd dangled and join them. "I can get a ride back," she threw over her shoulder.

She looked up and down the street for Dolores' car, the Honda she'd handed down to her sister last year. It wasn't anywhere to be seen. Yesenia tried not to read any meaning into that. Surely she could get a ride from Raul in his brand new Escalade if it came down to it.

Ignoring her, he beeped the locks and was by her side at the front door.

"Don't mention the condo deal, okay?" A single whiff

of her plans, and Mama would have her back in the house sleeping under a crucifix. After Cameron had signed the loan papers and the divorce papers, she'd planned to present it as a *fait accompli;* that was *if* she told her mother at all.

Quelling the acid eating away at the lining of her stomach, she knocked and entered. "Mama!"

"*Estoy en la cocina,*" came a shouted reply.

She followed the smell of cooking *empanadas.* Her mouth watered when the scents of Hidalgo pushed away the despair that had pooled in her belly moments ago.

"*¿De qué tipo los haces?*" she asked.

"*Pollo con papas —*" Whatever else her mother was going to say was cut off by the sight of Cameron filling the dining room archway.

Wiping her floured hands on an apron, her mother started in on him in Spanish.

"*En inglés, Mama,*" she implored. Mama gave her a look that said she was not happy at being accosted in her own house, and turned back to stuffing the chicken and potatoes in the thin pastry.

"Did I hear right?" Undoubtedly sensing the drama she thrived on, her sister Dolores was in the room in an instant. Yesenia didn't think she'd ever seen Dolores move that fast. Mellow was a gross understatement where her sister was concerned. "Long time no see," Dolores said.

Because she'd been the youngest when they'd arrived in southern California, Dolores' English was the best. Full of colloquial phrases Yesenia and Mama could never get quite right.

"Are you high?" Cameron asked. Pounding in her

head started in earnest. Yesenia and her mother had learned to studiously ignore the haze of marijuana smoke that always followed Dolores like dirt trailed Pigpen. With a pot dispensary on nearly every L.A. corner now, their little Dolores went prescription in hand, and got supplied weekly.

"You gonna call the cops on me?" she asked, draping her lanky frame across two of the black lacquer dining room chairs.

Cameron didn't say anything more, merely shook his head.

Ignoring the escalating pain in her temples, Yesenia jumped in to mediate. "Dori, don't."

"*Quizás La Migra, también,*" her mother added.

"*Mamá,* Cam's never called Immigration on us. Plus you know that he's bound by Special Order forty," she said, seeking out and finding pain reliever on the counter of the pass through. Yesenia helped herself to water from her mother's glass.

"Maybe you don't worry so much because you're legal," her mother added.

Nothing like guilt with lunch. Cameron's marriage to her had made her legal before the post 9/11 laws had gotten crazy restrictive. But after the INS had gone defunct and Homeland Security had taken over, Yesenia could no longer sponsor her family for citizenship as she'd planned. There'd been no hurry to start the paperwork way back then. What was another month or year, she'd thought when in the early throes of blissful marriage. Then, it had been too late.

The little Prado-Morales clan had all entered the

country illegally. And now Mama and Dolores were stuck
in undocumented limbo. Her own status made every
conversation one of her versus them.

She had the husband, the job, the ability to pass
through immigration checkpoints without harassment.
Yesenia's status weighed on her like chain mail on a worn
out medieval soldier. Buying them the house, giving
Dolores the car, giving them money. None of it really
absolved the guilt for more than a few months.

She turned to Cam, ready to ask the source of the
agitation between her and her family to leave, but the look
of defiance in his eyes quickly changed her mind. One
more argument, she didn't need.

Instead she pulled an apron from the nail on the wall
and made herself useful. Yesenia cut up avocados, peeled
tomatillos and chopped onions for the salsa. Working in
concert with her mother, like they had so many times
before, she pulled one pan of *pastes* out of the oven while
her mother moved to shove another in.

"Is *he* staying for lunch?" Dolores asked, floured finger
pointed toward Cam.

"I'm right here," Cam said, helping himself to a dining
room chair.

Dolores crossed her arms for a long moment. Yesenia
hid a smile. Did everyone in her life have to be so closed
off and defiant at the same time? It was funny when it
wasn't aggravating. When her mother lost the staring
contest with Cam, she directed Dolores to set another
place at the dining room table.

♥

JESSIE NIBBLED AT HER FOOD. Reina would have filled her daughter's plate ten times over if his ex ate at a normal rate. But the closer Jessie had gotten to the weeknight anchor desk, the more she nibbled at her mother's cooking.

"If you're not going to eat, talk to me," Reina said in English. The glare she gave him let him know she'd made a big accommodation for his benefit.

"What do you want to know, Mama?"

"How long were you stuck?" Dolores interjected.

He watched his wife's tan face lose its color for a moment. Then she caught herself.

"Two or three hours. Not too long." Cam refrained from coughing "bullshit" into his closed fist. She'd always minimized her troubles for her family's sake. He'd always told Jessie if they really knew the sacrifices she made for them, they'd appreciate what she did. Or at least meet her halfway, instead of relying on her to do all the heavy lifting.

Sparked by the smell of potential misery that wasn't her own, Dolores leaned forward. "Did you pass out?"

"No," Jessie snapped, uncharacteristically. "It was fine."

Dolores didn't miss a beat. Ignoring Jessie's discomfort, she leaned forward. "How did this one end up there?" Jessie's sister thrust an accusing thumb his way.

Flustered, Jessie didn't answer. In the old days he would have answered for her. Told Dolores to mind her own business, cut her sister some slack. But he was biding his time. He'd been doing a lot of thinking over the last twelve hours and this time, he planned to get Reina and Dolores on his side.

When he stopped thinking and planning and hoping, Dolores was coming back into the room, slick new iPad in hand. Unless Dolores had suddenly found gainful employment, it was an expensive toy for a perennially broke woman. That kind of gift was Raul Vega's calling card. Cameron hoped for all their sakes, that drug-dealing pimp wasn't back in the picture.

Dolores tapped and swiped at the screen, oblivious to his thoughts or her sister's discomfort. Ultimately, she pressed a small right facing arrow over a screen shot from a video.

He watched Jessie and himself coming out of the elevator. The woman in the video was doing her best to hide her strain, but he could see it clearly now. In the wrinkles around her eyes, in the tightness pulling at her mouth. He'd been so damn bowled over by being with his Jessie, that he hadn't recognized the tension. Under his lashes he looked from Dolores to Reina and back at Jessie.

They were so caught up in what Jessie's death would have meant for *them*, that they didn't see how the quake had affected *her*.

"Our own Yesenia Morales was a victim of the five point one quake," a voice said. This was replaced by video of him, arms crossed, standing in a corner. "LAPD Lieutenant Cameron Becker, Morales' husband, rescued her from the disabled elevator." The camera zoomed in on the earnest look she'd carefully arranged on her face. "This is the story in her own words."

He was only partially grateful the broadcast was in English. He could understand everything Jessie said, but listening to her hide the anguish in her voice twisted his gut.

Cam watched Jessie's family watch the rest of the video.

"All that expensive therapy worked then?" Dolores asked.

Jessie's sharp intake of breath was the only sign of her discomfort. "I did what was recommended," she said.

"Do you still take the drugs the doctors gave you?" Dolores asked.

"*Drogas son malísimas*," Reina interjected, shaking her head. Her thumbs-down stand on Jessie's use of prescription drugs didn't quite jibe with the smoke-permeated room of Dolores.

"I don't take the drugs anymore, Mama," Jessie said. "I'm using breathing and visualization techniques these days. As long as I stay off elevators, I'm fine for the most part."

He waited for them to ask what they could do to comfort her. Or to probe the other part that wasn't fine. But they didn't.

"Good thing all that therapy was worth it," Reina said not quite under her breath.

"I didn't ask you to come to the U.S., Mama."

"What was I supposed to do? You were dying there in Mexico. You couldn't leave the apartment. The doctors we were seeing there only gave you drugs that made you a zombie. I couldn't take care of you all day and work. *El coyote* promised good, free medical care on this side of the border. So I did what I had to do. What any mother would have done."

On that single thing, the *coyote* had been as good as his word.

"And you'll never let me forget it," Jessie said in an unusual show of defiance. Maybe she'd gotten some backbone in their years apart. He'd seen a little bit of it this morning, and more now.

"What is there to forget, *mija?* I uprooted my whole family for you. We don't expect anything in return, except a little help from time to time."

"Mama, I helped you buy this house. I pay some of the bills—"

"What about Dolores? She listened to you and went to Cal State. Took out those loans. But without papers, she can't get any kind of job. She needs help to get her green card."

"If I get a promotion, Mama, I'll be in a better position to help."

"If I get this job, Mama. If I get married, Mama. Nothing has changed but you."

Jessie looked at Dolores' eyes, pleading for someone to stand with her. But her sister said nothing, just rearranged her body for maximum comfort. Why couldn't they see that Jessie had gone above and beyond? They weren't doing anything to help themselves. His wife wasn't Superwoman.

"The *empanadas* were very good, Mrs. Prado," Cameron said, ready to get his wife the hell out of here before her family sucked the very life from her. Where he'd been annoyed this morning with her notions about buying a place, he could see now that she needed it. Needed somewhere and something to call her own. He wanted more for her. He wanted to be the one to give her what she required.

After a long commentary in Spanish, Dolores translated a single sentence. "Mama wants to know what you're really doing here."

He hadn't known why he was there an hour ago. But he was sure now. More sure than he'd been in years.

"I'm here to get my wife back."

FOUR

SHE WAS the frog in the pot, and someone had just turned up the heat.

"Oh. My. God. Seriously?" Dolores asked. "This is gonna be good," her sister said like they were in a South L.A. theater and had gotten to the good part.

"Did he say what I think he said?" Mama said to Dolores in Spanish.

"Sí, sí, Mamá," Dolores assured Mama.

She looked at her husband. "I can't believe you're doing this. You know this isn't what I want."

"You haven't given us a real chance," Cameron said. "And after last night—"

"What happened last night?" Dolores asked, looking like she was thinking about making popcorn for the public spectacle the end of their marriage had become.

"We've given this a thousand chances." She stood and gathered her bag. "Take me home, Cameron."

She needed to talk to him. But discussing her sex life

or their divorce in front of her mother and sister held little appeal.

"It was just getting good," Dolores whined in protest. If Yesenia had been twelve she'd have slapped her sister when their mother wasn't looking. Instead she used the only weapon she could.

She pulled her hand from the doorknob and locked eyes with her sister. "Where's the Honda?"

Dolores' mouth opened and closed like a goldfish starved for air. Mama got up and cleared the table with remarkable efficiency. Water splashed in the kitchen sink while she did dishes, loudly.

"Raul borrowed it."

Any sentence that included Raul Vega was trouble. She dropped her bag and leaned against the front door, defeat nailing her feet to the floor.

"And?"

"He said it got a little banged up. So he took it to his guy to fix it."

"You're telling me that Raul, who's driving a new Escalade —"

"It's a Panamera now."

"Excuse me, a new Porsche. Raul needed *my* car?"

Her sister squirmed. "You said I could have it."

"I said you could *use* it so you could look for a job, drive Mama around. And I shouldn't have even done that. You have no license. No insurance."

"The new law —"

"Hasn't taken effect yet," Cameron interjected.

The water shut off in the kitchen. Towel in hand, her mom came back to the dining room. "This is why she needs a green card. Without a job she gets up to no good."

"I don't know what more I can do right now," Yesenia said. Her shoes were glued to the floor. Any minute she expected the tug into the quicksand.

"If you move back here, that's two thousand a month we could pay *un abogado*."

In one deft move, their mother had turned the tables on her. Dolores doing something stupid with a car, one with Yesenia's name on the title and insurance, became a reason to move back home and sacrifice her autonomy.

Cameron's phone beeped. In that moment, she loved him more than she ever had. They'd agreed to set off their phones, or way back when, their pagers when family became too much. "Gotta get into the station. I'll drop you off."

Her mom and sister retreated. They may hate the police, but there was one LAPD salary they didn't jeopardize. "You'll be here for Sunday dinner?" Mama asked, her eyes pleading.

"If I don't have to go into KESP, of course," she said before escaping out the door with Cameron.

Avoiding lawn arguing again, she waited until they got into the car before she let loose.

"What in the hell was that back there? This morning we were calmly and civilly discussing divorce and then you announce you want to get back together. In front of my family. Why?"

"Let's talk at your place."

The mechanic that fixed cars on their street sped by them at top speed, taking one of his customer's cars for a test drive. She buckled her seat belt and kept mute, letting Cameron navigate out of her old neighborhood.

Tears clogged her throat. It took a mile to swallow. Another to get her breathing back to normal. She was in a tangled web that was getting stickier by the moment.

Cam's phone beeped again.

"I thought that last call was fake."

When they stopped at a red light, he looked down at the phone. "It was. This one's real, though."

He pulled over on San Vicente. He picked up the phone, dialed and listened to the voice on the other end. After a moment, he opened the driver's door and stepped out. The talking became more animated.

If she'd had antennae, they would have twitched. "What's going on?"

He didn't look her way. Instead he returned to the seat and turned the wheel like the power steering had short circuited, crossing three lanes of traffic. Startled drivers blared their horns.

Cam had surprisingly little to say in the last ten minutes of their drive.

"You gonna be okay?" he asked at her front door. In better control than she'd been hours ago, she found her keys and twisted them in the lock.

"We're not getting back together."

"Jess...I can't do this." He pulled the phone from his pocket. Looked at it. Typed something. Shoved it back in.

"Why not? You can't cut and run like this. Are you even going to sign the papers?"

"Something's happening on a case, Jess. You of all people know I need to do what I can to—"

"Not you too. First my mother, then my sister, and now you. Because somehow every damn thing that happens is my fault. Why do you even want to try again if I've made your life a living hell and you don't trust me?"

"Who says I don't trust you?"

"What's the case you're working on?" It was the flicker of his eyes that snuffed out the tiny flame of hope she may have harbored. "Go to work, Cam."

"What about us?"

"There is no us. I'll send you the papers. Please sign them and send them back. After this place closes, I'll see a lawyer about the divorce. Don't fight me on this, please."

With one foot in her apartment and the other out the door, she saw Cam hesitate. But in the end, he did what he'd always done. He chose the force.

She closed the door behind him, ready to get on with her new life.

♥

CAMERON HAD TO PEE. Hydrate was the buzz word of the minute. Desert-dwelling Angelenos were suffering dehydration, department memos warned. Bottled water was everywhere. So he'd gotten into the habit of drinking, and drinking, and drinking. Now he had to go like a racehorse. Unlike a racehorse, though, he couldn't let loose while walking, oblivious to the world around him. Laughter escaped his lips. Jessie's nightly news could lead with, "Vice cop indecently exposes himself while on stakeout." But in Spanish. That would kill his career dead for sure. No one got a third chance.

Rivera put down her binoculars and turned her head his way. "What's so funny?"

"Nothing. Gotta go." They'd long ago made a cross-gender pact not to use plastic urine bottles in the car unless it was absolutely necessary.

She pulled a folded paper from her pant pocket. "Go to this motel. New owner's legit. Renting by the night and not the hour. He'll let you use the john."

He made a quick exit, snaking around the corner to the back of the motel. The skin and drug trade swirled around him. Everyone was too busy avoiding eye contact to notice him. A white Honda raced by on a mission. Something about the car looked familiar. He almost pulled out his phone to snap a pic of the plate when it pulled in to park, but his bladder got the better of him. Probably wasn't anything. At one time the car had been the best-selling vehicle in the US. Everyone from the rich to the poor drove that damned vehicle.

Got the key from the grateful owner and relieved himself. No more water tonight. No one got dehydrated sitting on their butt.

"Saw your wife's rescue," Rivera said before he could close the door good and tight.

"I thought you were keeping your kids away from the news."

"They went to soccer practice with their dad. Got an eyeful of you and Yesenia with my morning coffee."

Cameron opened another bottle of water. Took a swig. Anything not to have this conversation. But Rivera stuck her nose in anyway. "She ready to divorce you?"

"As a matter of fact, she is."

"Good."

"I don't want it."

If eyes could talk, Rivera's would have called him ten times a fool. She lifted the binoculars to her eyes and peered down the street. In a split second he was back in a different car or a different darkened street on a different night.

Rivera had been looking through similar binoculars, but there'd been nothing to see. The warehouse that had been the Wednesday night hotspot for betting and cock-fighting was as empty as a beggar's pocket and as silent as a tomb.

He'd flipped through his notebook making sure they were in the right place.

"They must have gotten a whiff of what was going down," Rivera had said.

"We have a mole?"

"Don't know. But let's call the Lieut and see what we should do."

But they'd never made that call to their superior. Instead the call had come in that they were to see the Deputy Police Chief immediately.

No time to change into civilian clothes or uniform, they'd come in looking like cat burglars and smelling like burgers, burritos, and piss.

If there had been any more brass in the room, the LAPD could have started a marching band. They were ordered to sit and someone had pressed a remote. The hiss of magnetic tape on spindles had filled the room, then he'd seen Jessie on TV.

For a long moment, he'd thought that someone was

playing an elaborate joke on them. Then he'd looked at Rivera and realized it was no practical joke.

Jessie was standing outside the same warehouse he'd just vacated. But this time, there was a swarm of activity. Birds squawked and flapped. Men scattered like roaches in broad daylight. And Jessie stood there yelling toward Christian Brooks, the star of TV's most popular sit com, *Temporary Family*.

"Sergeant Becker," the Deputy Chief had started. He knew what was coming. The weight of it hit his chest like a fist. "Are you married to Yesenia Morales?"

"Yes."

"Did you give her confidential information regarding this six-month long investigation?"

He took a long time to answer. And if he'd had it to do again, he'd have asked for his union rep. But he was young and stupid and in love. "Inadvertently."

It hadn't mattered at all what he'd said after that. He and Rivera had been separated. That night he'd begun his year long acquaintance with Internal Affairs. On the other end of that year, he bought sturdy shoes and walked the beat, alternating between downtown skid row and the seedy side of Hollywood Division.

"Earth to Becker." Fingers snapped in front of his face, bringing him to the present. Rivera talked into her radio, then to him. "Got a twenty on a situation."

"What's up?"

"Black SUVs are rolling in."

The city fleet. Los Angeles council members had drivers who took them to various events around the city's very spread out four hundred plus square miles. The

mayor being who he was had an LAPD officer chauf-
feuring him around. The council members being who they
were had to fund drivers from their own budget. In political speak, it gave them accountability for not wasting the
taxpayers' money. In real terms, it gave them discretion.
Rumor had it at least two of their illustrious city represen-
tatives had an appetite for prostitutes.

Which was why Cameron, years out from this kind of
grueling work was back at it again. Like any political
organization, the leadership had changed. And the mentor
he'd had out of the academy was one of the top brass now.
That meant forgiveness was in order, his good work on
earlier busts was recognized, and his one indiscretion set
aside.

If he did this one right, by the book, and made some
righteous busts he'd been promised that his career would
get back on track. So he was sitting, bladder nearly empty,
field glasses in hand, ready to bust this one wide open.

"Got him," Rivera exclaimed. She tucked the pocket
sized video camera between the seats. "Let's go," she
directed into the handheld radio.

Cameron, Rivera, and six other undercover vice cops
moved out of position. They all hightailed it to Hollywood
Boulevard.

The working women knew the score and weren't much
of a challenge. They never ran. He left them to the officers
who weren't in academy fit shape and ran after the high-
priced johns.

Rarely did he see out of shape middle-aged men run as
fast Olympic sprinters but shiny badges and fear of exposure were adrenaline.

The exhilaration of the hunt coupled with the specter of exoneration from his past mistakes kept his legs moving as he closed in on the man, his silver hair glinting under the streetlights of Lanewood Avenue.

He barreled into the other man with all his weight. They both went down.

"L.A.P.D." he ground out between breaths. "You're under arrest." He pulled out one of the zip cuffs he'd looped on his belt and pulled them tight.

He marched the perp back to Sunset where the patrol wagon should have been situated by now. He gave the guy the eyeball under the first street light they came upon. Wasn't Mitch Rasmussen, the council member they were looking to bust. But the guy wasn't chump change either.

"You Palmer Clemens?"

The heir apparent to a soon-to-be vacated council seat nodded. "I was only driving."

That remained to be seen. He continued to the main drag where thankfully the van was waiting.

"Everybody caught?" he called out to another officer.

The officer nodded and gave him the thumbs up. For the first time that night, Cameron breathed easier. He handed Clemens off and spotted Rivera.

She joined him next to their car.

"They doing Mirandas?" she asked.

"Yeah." Cameron had come to get his notepad. He needed names and birthdates of the arrestees. "I'll get the particulars," he said, thinking past the high of the initial bust about what it took to build a real case, one that would hold up in court.

He made a mental note to get all the info he could.

He'd call it in, get the paperwork in motion. Demotions aside, he'd been on the force too long to wrangle with the ever-changing computer system. That's what wet behind the ears officers were for. His mind strayed from details to the scene around him. This case would be made by the people in the van. But he didn't want to miss something big around him. Then a car caught his eye.

Rivera poked him in the shoulder. "What are you looking at, space case?"

"It's that Honda parked across the street. Can you make out the license plate?"

Rivera retrieved her field glasses and recited the string of numbers. Something about it sounded familiar, but he didn't want to leave the perps on ice too long.

"Can you run that plate?" he asked.

She nodded, already slipping into the vehicle and messing with the computer.

He opened the door of the patrol wagon with a slam. Despite being handcuffed to their seats, they jumped. Good.

"Listen up. Names, birthdates, socials. Don't lie. You'll only end up in lockup longer," he barked.

Rivera came in. Their communication was a wordless nod. She took one side, he the other. The first girl wouldn't even look up. He resisted looking at his watch. Processing better not take all night. He was looking forward to a beer, SportsCenter, and thoughts of Jessie. "Name."

She mumbled something. An older woman, who looked tweaked out, nudged the girl—hard. The woman needed to get fingerprinted, sprung, and back to work.

The LAPD had eaten into her profits. She shoved a skinny leg against the perp. The young girl tossed her long brown hair from her face defiantly and finally locked eyes with him.

"Dolores Morales."

Cameron nearly swayed in his boots. Not twelve hours ago, he'd been standing in a house watching this girl lay across the furniture as high as a kite.

No matter that this wasn't his fault, Jessie was going to kill him. Any chance of getting back together had just gone up in smoke. He wanted to pull Dolores aside, find out what in the hell she'd gotten wrapped up in. For his wife, he might have even let her go on the sly. But it was far too late. Everyone had seen her from the patrol officers to Rivera.

"Address?" His voice was flat.

"Think you know that."

The junkie next to Dolores, seeing an opportunity, suddenly looked sober. "You all know each other?"

He looked at his pad and scratched down the address of the home that he co-owned. He didn't ask her social because she didn't have one.

Cameron finished the last two women and peered at the faces on the other side of the van. Raul Vega wasn't anywhere to be seen. Good thing. He would have killed that little son of a bitch. This crap had his fingerprints all over it. Another vice cop pulled at him.

"I'm done. What's up?"

"Couple of undocumented here. Someone from USCIS will meet us down at the station."

Cameron shoved his notebook in his pocket, jumped

from the back of the van and slammed the door on his future. A misdemeanor was one thing. Possible detention care of Homeland Security was another matter altogether.

That beer and bed was a long ways away.

♥

"YOU HAVE A COLLECT CALL FROM...DOLORES Morales. This call is from a correctional facility," an automated voice interspersed with her sister reciting her name.

Sopa seca hit the floor. Noodles, cheese, and red sauce spread out on the tiles like small animal entrails. Her sister was in trouble. Its inevitability didn't make the reality any easier. Dolores was going to be deported. Yesenia would have to face her mother and take the blame. Through the interminable staticky delay, she gripped the phone for dear life, stepping over the food into the dining area.

"Yesenia!" her sister's yell came through the phone's earpiece.

"Dolores..." Yesenia paused to swallow the bile rising bitter in her throat. "What happened?"

"Cameron arrested me."

How could he do it? Arrest her sister. Better than anyone, he understood what would happen if she got arrested. He'd seen it happen a thousand times. They'd talked about it again and again, between themselves and with her sister. But Dolores hadn't given up Raul or her daily marijuana habit. Yet Yesenia had comforted herself with nothing more than an illusion of safety. But Dori and Mama had never been safe. And what little security they'd shared, Cameron had crushed tonight.

Their tacit agreement had been shattered. If he saw Dolores, he was supposed to look the other way. If as Cameron said, the cops turned a blind eye to the illegal activities of celebrities and their kids, politicians and their kids, not to mention the consulates and their kids, hadn't her sister deserved at least that little bit of consideration from her brother-in-law even if he was a soon to be ex? All the thoughts turned her brain to mush.

"Where are you?" Yesenia asked, making a monumental effort to keep panic at bay.

"Hollywood division."

"I'll be right there." Leaving the phone dangling and the food for the ants, she shoved her feet into her boots and sped to Hollywood in less than ten minutes.

She eyed the desk sergeant. "I need to see —"

"I've got this," Cameron said, elbowing the other officer out of the way and entering the lobby through a side door.

"I can't believe —"

His voice and grip were steel. "Not here," he said and steered her through a door and toward what looked like an interrogation room, if the chairs bolted to the floor and the cuff tie down loops were any indication.

She took the initiative and slammed the door. Leaning against it, she drew in four deep breaths. Interlacing her fingers, she clasped her hands together behind her back. Doing violence to an LAPD officer in a police station would not turn out well, no matter how much provocation she could prove.

"I didn't know it was her," he explained.

That was his opening gambit? "You've known Dolores a dozen years, but you couldn't pick her out of a crowd?"

"She had her—"

"Please don't tell me you think we all look alike. I *never* thought you were that—"

"Hey. *Hey*," he said, walking right up to Yesenia, not leaving even an inch between. Forced her to look up. "Don't ever say that again. I'm not that guy. I was never that guy. You know who I am, Yesenia. I treat everyone fairly, no matter what."

His eyes pierced hers. Cameron didn't look away until she gave him a nod acknowledging his truth.

"I was chasing another perp. Patrol officers loaded the wagon. I didn't see her until she was cuffed," he explained.

"What are you going to do?" Let her out was the only acceptable response.

"We have to process her," he said. Wrong answer.

"Cameron, she'll be in ICE detention before the week is up." Dolores could be in some anonymous lockup for months or years. On a bus to Tijuana or worse after that.

"You don't know that," he said with equanimity.

"What was she arrested for?"

Cameron backed away, striding to the other side of the small room. He looked at the two-way window as if he could see what was on the other side, when she knew he couldn't. He was avoiding her.

"I work in vice." He left the rest unsaid. Prostitution? It couldn't be. Dolores did a lot of stupid things. But never that. If it had been illegal betting, he would have said that. Dog fighting? Vice was everything decent people liked to sweep under the rug.

Her stomach formed a hard knot in the middle of her body.

"Tell me. Is this why you had to rush out this afternoon?"

"Off the record?" His tone was flat.

That stung like a wasp. "This is about family, not work."

"I made the mistake of believing that before," he said.

Weary, she sat in one of the metal chairs. "How is it you think we can get back together, have a future if you don't trust me?"

Pulling himself from the reflective glass, he sat across from her, clasping his hands together like the nuns had made her as a child in Mexico. "We belong together."

"Because we made the mistake of standing together in church before God?"

"It wasn't a mistake, Jessie."

"Do you even love me? Or is this all part of your big sense of obligation?"

Cameron stood, paced to the door and back. He'd never been demonstrative out of bed. Now she wondered if all he saw was a big responsibility when he looked at her. He'd married her, and her family. Romance hardly figured into it when you looked at it that way.

Back and forth, he walked. She knew that posture. He was churning things over in his mind. Making a decision.

When he sat back down, he covered her hands with his. That simple touch did more to repair the rift between them than words ever could.

"You know who Mitch Rasmussen is?" It was both a question and statement.

"The fourth district councilman. Mostly Hancock Park and Hollywood."

"He solicits prostitutes."

"In public?" The arrogance and stupidity of politicians she would never understand.

"The tenth district guy is involved as well. We've been building a case for a few months. Rasmussen's been using his city car, city employees, and public money."

"How does Dolores fit in?"

"Raul runs girls and drugs now."

"And Dolores helps him. How?"

"Her...*your*...car was at the scene."

"Let me talk to her." She knew her request probably broke all rules and regulations. Cameron never flouted them. She put her hands on top, squeezed his. "*¿Por favor? Mi familia es mi mundo,*" she whispered.

His chair scraped against the cement floor, shattering intimacy. He stepped out, locking her in.

All these months and years later, she could finally admit the bare naked truth to herself. She'd made a mistake. Her ambition had been the straw that broke the back of their divorce. A single mistake. Until today, she'd believed Cam had never forgiven her. Maybe all wasn't lost. That tiny flame of hope flickered again.

Memories she'd long tucked away into a corner of her mind came back in full force. When they'd been living together as man and wife, she and Cam had always swapped war stories. The ability to speak freely about work had been one of the strongest bricks of the foundation of their marriage.

"Are you close to arrest?" she had asked him a year before their marriage would end.

"You know I can't talk about this, Jessie," he'd said.

"I'm not probing," she'd said. "I want you home at night." Her tone left no doubt as to the reason she wanted him home. They had been close in this other way. He'd embraced her desire for him, nurtured it, helped it bloom.

"We're close. It's been a crap assignment," he said.

Dinner done and dishes washed, she'd come from the kitchen and sat on his lap. "Anything I can do?" She massaged his shoulders, trying to rub some of the tension from the taut muscles.

"I wish I could scrub it from my head."

"What? Tell me." She'd never thought there was a story there. She'd only wanted to share her husband's obvious anguish.

"Cockfighting. Hundreds of people follow these birds fighting around Los Angeles."

"Seriously?" she asked. Of course she'd heard about it, but in the same conversation as dog fighting. She ignored it though, despite the early morning crowing of cocks and late night barking pit bulls in the neighborhood where she and Dori had grown up.

"They add spurs and gaffs." Cameron went on to describe how the roosters were accessorized to tear each other to pieces. How the ring runners bagged hundreds of dead birds a weekend. She looked away then, trying to cleanse images from her own imagination.

Their conversation hadn't been more than those few words. They'd spent the weekend creating new memories. Despite Cameron's demands for an explanation, she could never pinpoint what had spurred her to mention it at a pitch meeting. Her old boss at KESP had told her to run with the story. Next thing she knew she was assigned to the story. It was a big coup when she'd uncovered a popular sit-com star was a big better in the ring.

She'd had a special seat at the anchor desk, reporting the five minute long package. Animal rights activists made the story viral. The nation had been rightly horrified by the actor's extracurricular activities, and the sit-com had promptly been cancelled after viewers boycotted it. The night after her story had aired, Cameron had come home early and furious.

"You're home early," she'd broached tentatively.

"My investigation's done."

"That's good," she'd started.

"No, Jessie. Not good. Rivera and I got pulled from the investigation. The cock fighting sting is over. We're the subject now."

Yesenia didn't think she'd done anything wrong, exactly. But her stomach started sinking, nonetheless. "I don't understand."

He came closer, his size intimidating. "What don't you get? You reported on the ring. The organization guys disappeared. There's no one to arrest."

"What about the actor?"

"That guy? He'll never be arrested. The LAPD doesn't go after celebrities unless it's drunk driving or murder. It's the top guys we needed to shut it down."

Her voice went quiet. "Don't you still know who they are?"

Cam whistled. "They're long gone. Evidence has been destroyed. Three months of work down the drain."

He'd stormed off. Never a big talker, Cameron had shut her out after that. For six months, their conversations had been monosyllabic exchanges. Seeing the writing on the wall, she'd acted on her family's advice and had filed for separation.

All their differences about her family and his had crowded out whatever love had been there. That single breach of trust had been the reason their marriage had failed. She quelled the urge to call Ernesto. She would not breach his trust again, even if their marriage was on the verge of extinction.

Nearly thirty minutes later, Yesenia was starting to consider whether claustrophobia was something else to add to her list of irrational fears, when a uniformed officer brought Dori in.

Though the officer locked the door, she didn't think for one minute she and her sister were alone. But she didn't care who was listening. As far as Yesenia could tell, Dolores didn't have a damned thing to lose.

"Are you selling yourself now?" She asked in English. Dori always took her more seriously when Yesenia spoke their second language.

"I can't believe you'd think that." Dolores at once looked defeated and offended.

"Where were you?"

"On Hollywood Boulevard. I was walking La Brea to Sunset." The pause was longer than the quake they'd recently suffered, and nearly as scary. "With Raul."

Jesus, Mary, and Joseph. Raul had a big TV, a big car,

big dreams, but no honest means of income she'd ever
been able to decipher. When they'd finally found a house
they could afford, she'd almost backed out of the deal
when Raul Vega had sauntered between the adjoining
yards. Like God's gift to women, he'd hit on all three of
them. Only Dolores had taken the bait.

"Can you get Cameron to let me out?"

Yesenia didn't know if she could ask that, again.
Cameron didn't violate his principals. It's one of the things
she'd loved about him. He could always be counted on to
do the right thing. She shook her head, making a decision
not to ask him to do that. If he did anything on Dolores'
behalf, it would have to be of his own volition.

"But he loves you." Dori's voice was a plea. "He
always has. You know that. This is only one little favor."

"This is not little, Dolores. What will it take for you to
leave Raul alone?"

"He's all I have."

"Are you serious? You have Mama. And you
have me."

"No one has you but you. You left for Cameron, for
KESP. Sure, you see Mama once a week. But you've
forgotten what it's like living there. To be the embodiment of Dad's memory. I don't even remember Papa. But
I look like him and speak like him. And have done
nothing with all the opportunities you and Mama have
given me."

"Oh, Dori—"

"Don't 'Oh, Dori' me. You got to leave, but I can't. I
live in the house you pay for. I drive the car you handed
down."

"Life in America has been hard. Maybe Mexico would have been worse. I don't know. But why Raul?"

"He's all the things you think he is. He sells weed and crystal."

"Girls?"

"I…" Dolores looked away. "Someone high up asked Raul to work with a few girls, supplying them with drugs, giving them protection. I was helping with the business end of things."

"Raul is legal, you're not. Didn't you think about what could happen?"

"I thought you'd be glad I was using my degree."

If she'd stayed home that day with her mother and Dori. If they'd taken the earlier elevator. None of this would have happened. There was no going back, but forward had caused nothing but misery.

She looked at her sister. Yesenia pulled the phone from her purse and set it on the table between them. "We're going to have to call Mama."

But they didn't. Neither of them reached for that phone, lying between them like nuclear waste. That gave them a few minutes to plot out the next few days. While Dori sulked, Yesenia was contemplating just what she could get Cam to do for her within the bounds of the law. The doorknob jiggled, and the object of her thoughts appeared as if she'd made him materialize.

"She's free to go," he said to them. "Take your sister home. Get her a lawyer."

"How?" she asked, grateful not to have had to put his loyalty to the test.

"Dolores is not a threat to national security."

"But—"

"I have to go process the real criminals, and get ready for—" He turned red, a mean feat for the man. "Nothing. Take her home."

Was he embarrassed he'd done them a favor? She wanted to know more about that face, but couldn't look a gift horse in the mouth.

Involuntary detention was no joking matter. Their mother had told some hair raising tales of neighbors who'd disappeared. It made a crappy bus ride to Tijuana sound like vacation.

They didn't talk much on the long ride down Highland, then La Brea. They settled on a single thing, though.

"Don't tell Mama," Dolores had implored the minute they left the station.

Yesenia hated lying, but on this one they agreed. "Of course not. She'd have a heart attack ten times over."

"You'll help me?" Dolores' voice got small for the second time that night. Yesenia wanted to take Cam's age-old advice and practice tough love. Tell her sister no for once. Make her ask Raul for the damned money.

She wouldn't do any of that. The money she'd put away for a down payment on her condo would go to helping her sister any way it could.

"*Cameron salió en la televisión,*" Mama said as soon as they got through the security door. She was so relieved that Mama hadn't asked where they were or why they'd come home together, that it took a few seconds for her words to sink in.

Cameron on television? What? Yesenia ran to the

living room, and her husband's face loomed larger than life on the ancient projection screen.

"We have breaking news. A channel Five exclusive. A warrant for the arrest of fourth district councilman Mitch Rasmussen has been issued by the Los Angeles Police Department," the reporter started. Video of police officers, their reflective vests glowing, filled the screen. A dozen perps being marched to the wagon. "This ends the month long city council corruption sting."

He'd hesitated to tell her something the LAPD was all too happy to share with Channel Five?

For a short few moments, when her sister had been returned to her custody, she'd thought Cameron had changed. That he'd finally placed some trust in her to make the right decisions. A tiny inkling of hope had started to spring up. Maybe they *could* have tried again.

It was the same old crap. He didn't trust her. She had changed, but he hadn't noticed.

FIVE

DISCRETION WAS what had allowed him to let Dolores go without notifying the feds. One less Mexican face on the bus to ICE detention had gone unnoticed. Discretion was what had pushed him to make his conversation with Yesenia off-the-record even if it wasn't strictly necessary. It had been a test, a stupid one. But he wanted reassurance that she'd keep a hot story to herself.

Both ways, he was damned.

It was stupid, but he'd expected Jessie to call. He'd put his heart out there, and it had been rebuffed. With a sister facing jail and possible deportation, it was silly to think she'd be thinking about his proposal that they get back together. But he'd been stupidly hopeful.

They'd come together the night of the earthquake because that's what people did when they faced death. Their bodies called for them to create life. After fear had worn off, everything had gone back to the way it had been. Jessie hadn't even called him about the condo.

When they came, he'd sign the papers no matter what.

If he'd learned anything in the last few days it was that she needed a place of her own, separate from Reina's smothering and Dolores' recriminations.

And what he needed, if he wanted his wife back, was a plan. Which was how he found himself answering the door for his brother. Desperate times and all that.

"Hey, bro," Ryan said. His brother initiated that guy hug/handshake combo—awkwardly. Cameron wanted to bust his brother's chops, tell him macho stuff wasn't Ryan's thing. But he didn't want to insult the guy when he needed his help.

"Um, have a seat," said Cam. Maybe he shouldn't throw stones. He was the awkward one now. He let out a big sigh. He wasn't a talker. His day job didn't require much talking. Neither did his civilian life. But this asking for advice thing did.

In a thousand years, he'd never, ever seen himself doing this. But Ryan had two things Cam didn't: a girl-friend, and the planning gene. His brother had planned out his life, career. The man didn't make a single decision without listing the pros and cons on a pad and deliberating.

Ryan looked around before taking a seat. "No game on?"

Cam lifted the remote and reluctantly turned on ESPN. He could take or leave sports. But it was the perfect time filler when you had no regular woman. And it kept people from talking too much, asking him too many questions. After fifteen minutes of larger than life men chasing after balls, he lowered the volume, watching the lighted squares disappear one by one from the bottom of the screen.

With degrees from Stanford and the University of Chicago, Ryan was no dummy. "What?" his brother asked, looking straight ahead, sparing Cam his uncomfortable scrutiny.

"I need a plan," Cam admitted.

"What do you want?" Ryan asked, pulling a yellow pad from the messenger bag at his feet. He clicked a ballpoint pen, poised to write.

"Get my wife back."

Click.

The pen went back into the chamber. Cam could feel his brother's eyes boring into his head. He watched Jade McCarthy's lips move, followed by a video clip from a game. Ryan grabbed for the remote, muting it when a commercial for chips filled all fifty-five inches of the screen.

Then he looked at Cam. "Are you serious?"

"I'd kind of been thinking about it. Then she called me."

"The quake?"

"Yeah."

"How's her family?"

"Not good."

"Quake damage?"

"Not exactly."

"What do they need now?"

Cam wanted to cry foul, protest that Ryan's question was unfair. But it was completely fair. His brother had helped iron out the legalities of the house purchase for Reina and Dolores. He'd referred them to any number of lawyers who all doled out the same advice. There were few paths to citizenship for those who entered the country without papers. But they needed more than money this time around.

"Dolores got arrested."

"Jesus. Couldn't have been a surprise, though. What is Jessie asking you to do?"

"It's not like that."

"What, she didn't ask you for a favor?"

Cam didn't want Jessie to be the only one tarred with a brush. "I arrested her."

Ryan sucked air through his teeth. Held up his hands. "I don't need the details. Does she need a lawyer?"

"I can't get involved this time. Big conflict of interest."

"And you want to dip your toe in this water again?"

"Watch it, bro."

"Your marriage was the Titanic."

"We were young. Didn't handle things well. We've matured. People change."

"That's putting lipstick on a pig," Ryan said, not an ounce of diplomacy in sight. His voice softened, which made Cam want to punch him. "You're my brother. I want what's best for you. Now that I've found someone—"

"Spare me the single guy pity party. Are you gonna help me or not?"

"How are you going to handle her all-encompassing ambition? Did you forget she cost you two years of your career? Remember the winter it rained nearly every day while you walked a beat in Hollywood? Working the night shift. All the while she clawed her way from reporter to weekend anchor?"

"She's got weeknights."

"Will that be enough? There's bigger local, national. Hell, international now."

Ryan wasn't wrong. "The past is the past for a reason. She didn't run with the Rasmussen story."

"You told her?"

"I'm learning to trust her."

"You still love her." It was a statement, not a question. Cam didn't feel any compulsion to respond.

"How did you know Sophie was the girl for you? 'Cause to my way of thinking, you seem like oil and water."

Deflection worked the same in his living room as it worked in the interrogation room. Ryan went red to the roots of his hair. But he did what Cam needed him to do. He picked up the pad again.

When the seriousness of the occasion penetrated Ryan's snark, they moved to the dining room table.

"Did you do this for Sophie?"

Ryan played obtuse. "What?"

"Make a plan?"

His brother turned tomato red again. "It had eleven points."

"Like?" Maybe he could borrow one or two. Didn't need to reinvent the wheel.

"Not gonna share that. Let's get back to *your* plan."

His brother had never been too good at sharing. Baby of the family was like that. "Fine."

"What worked in your marriage?"

This was going to be easy. "Put sex on the top of that list, bro."

"Been on this earth long enough to know you're gonna need more than the magic in your pants."

"That's why you're here."

Ryan clicked his pen officiously. "Did you tell her you love her?"

He didn't need his brother. He had this. "She knows."

"C'mon man. You know better than that."

His brain was starting to hurt. Palm on forehead, he rubbed at his temples. Maybe he needed a beer. "How so?"

"Have you ever told her?" his brother asked.

"Not in so many words." He stood. Paced the room. It was getting hot in the studio apartment. Maybe he should open a window.

"She needs those words," Ryan persisted.

He gripped the back of the chair where he'd been sitting. "Where'd you learn this? Mom never says she loves us. But you know she does."

"She used to say it when we were kids," Ryan said, his voice going quiet. "Dad used to tell her he loved her all the time."

Cam spun the chair around. Sat on it backwards. He remembered that. His dad had always been kissing his mom, tickling her in the kitchen. It had made him uncomfortable when he was nine. Made him squirmy now. "Only made it harder when he died."

They were quiet a long time. Their mom had suffered when their father had died. The loss of the stability a good income brought and a father for her kids had been one thing. The loss of the man had devastated her for years. She never dated. He didn't know if she was over it now. Wasn't something he was ever going to ask her about, though.

Ryan scratched in *love* as number two.

"What did Jessie want you to change when you guys were together?"

"Be nicer to her family."

"You bought them a house," he said, but wrote in *family*. "You need something more concrete. You're gonna have to talk to her, show her why it works."

Cam rolled his neck from one side to another. Shoulder shrugs down in the gym were probably making his muscles tight. "Like what?"

"Make her dinner. Learn more Spanish. Smooth things over with our mom."

"Bridget?" His mom hadn't picked his friends in over thirty years. He certainly wasn't interested in her picking a wife.

"She thinks Jessie used you. Needed you, but didn't love you."

"She told you that?"

"More than once," Ryan said. "And Jessie knows that. Mom didn't hide her feelings. You should probably add standing up to Mom to your list."

Cam grunted. He should have stood up to his mom, but had done the cowardly thing and let Jessie handle it. Damn, he'd fucked this up ten ways to Sunday.

"It's not that she didn't like Jessie," Ryan continued. "She didn't like Jessie for you."

"Does she like Sophie for you?" Ryan's girl wasn't traditional by any stretch of the imagination.

"Yeah, mostly. You saw they get along. I think she'd be happier if Sophie wanted to get married. But I'm okay where it is."

"Are you?" He didn't believe that for a moment. Ryan had already been engaged once. He was built for marriage and babies and kids. They both were.

"For now."

"Why she'd want to marry a guy with a soccer dad car, I don't know."

"It's a sport sedan."

"Two words that should never be together."

Ryan shoved him. Cam looked at his brother. "I can take you."

"We ended at a draw," Ryan said, throwing down the gauntlet.

"Brother wars," they said simultaneously before they hit the floor. Not a few seconds later, Cameron had him in a half nelson hold.

"No fair, you can't use police maneuvers," Ryan said from underneath him.

"You didn't call it."

"Get me a beer," Ryan said. Cam let him up and they retreated to the couch and CNN, because the guest got to pick the channel.

Two hours after Ryan left, Cam turned off the third rerun of SportsCenter. The anchors were talking about some crazy people who cycled a hundred miles a day. That wasn't a sport to watch. That was torture.

The single sheet of yellow paper, held down by a single

salt shaker beckoned. He read it again, committing it to memory. Follow these five steps, and maybe, possibly, Yesenia and he might have a chance.

Step one was for him to call her, wherein, Ryan's word, the rest would fall into line like cops on parade. Cam could get with that. Step four even made him blush. He had to smile a little. Maybe there was hope. He tucked the paper back under the salt, and went to find his phone.

Before Jessie could speak, he told her, "If you bring over the papers, I'll sign them."

❦

CLUTCHING HER PURSE CLOSE, Yesenia looked up toward the roof of the building.

Three floors.

It figured that Cameron would be on the top. Those third-floor apartments had balconies. Everyone wanted to be high up in Los Angeles. She found it ironic for people living in such a squat city. Taking a deep breath, she drove into the parking structure looking for visitor parking. Of course, the designated path led straight from the car to the elevator bay.

All people talked about in southern California was staying in shape. Despite the local obsession with fitness, however, finding the stairs for any building was always a challenge. She looked right, then left, found and followed the exit signs. A sigh of relief escaped her lips when she pushed open the door and no alarm screamed. She'd learned early after arriving in L.A. that the tallest buildings had fire alarms triggered by open doors. One stern lecture from a very pissed off L.A. firefighter and she mostly adhered to the warnings.

She quickly made her way up the flights and to Cameron's door. Standing on his doormat, she hesitated. Yesenia reviewed her agenda one last time. He'd said he'd sign the papers and share dinner. She didn't have the papers anymore. That dream was on hold, but she did need to drive the train tonight.

First, she needed his advice on what to do about Dori. Second, they needed to have a frank discussion about divorce and the future. He'd said he wanted to get back together, but she couldn't see a future with someone who didn't trust her judgment. She'd made a mistake, a whopper of an error. But she'd grown and learned. Putting her off the Mitch Rasmussen story still stung.

Ernesto hadn't hid his disappointment that KESP had somehow been overlooked when press had been assembled. She'd been right in the belly of the beast, so to speak, and hadn't caught a whiff of the biggest scandal to hit municipal government that year.

As if she were a paparazza with no discretion, Cameron had shut her out. Never again would she be so stupid as to compromise a police investigation to break a story. But she would never ignore something she thought the public had a right to know about. Her arm ached, perched as it was between knocking and hanging by her side.

She needed only to remember they didn't want the same things. Cam probably had some misguided notion that having sex once made it so they should get back together. She wanted him. Yesenia banged her knuckles against her head, banishing the thought. She was human. The sex was good. But what she needed was help for Dolores. That had to be her top priority. All throbbing and tingling was to be ignored.

Before she could form another fist and make her presence known, Cameron pulled open the door. That uncanny sixth sense he'd had about her must have alerted him. She didn't even pretend to be surprised. Instead she registered that a bottle of wine was in his other hand. She looked at his waist. He was wearing an apron. Yesenia tried to rearrange things in her brain. Humans craved order. In her job, she'd learned that no matter what happened to people, they strove to make sense of their surroundings. None of this made sense.

"You're cooking?" she asked, straining to keep the incredulity from her voice.

"I've changed."

Boy, had he. She couldn't remember him doing anything more than scrambling eggs. Ryan cooked, but Cameron ate. It's what had always made Ryan a great catch. The more promising of the two brothers. But she'd fallen for this strong, silent one who didn't cook, clean or do laundry.

Yesenia looked around. There was only a single huge room. The kitchen was in one corner, the living room in another. The dining area and the freshly made king-size filled out the other two. The sheer modesty curtain did little to obscure the bed.

The TV was off. That was another difference. Between the constant sports games or replays on ESPN and KESP news or CNN, they'd had the set on nearly twenty-four hours a day when they'd lived together. She'd sometimes hated it. But its constant flickering presence made avoiding arguments much easier. Instead of talking about her mother's constant visits or his mother's coldness toward her, they could stare at the television and maintain civility. She longed to find the remote and turn it on.

"*What* are you making?" she asked, enticed by the smells coming from the apartment.

"Lemon, parmesan, and pine nut crumb pork escalopes," he read from a note card on the counter.

Remembering her manners, she offered, "Do you need help?"

"No, have a seat." He pointed to the couch. She pulled off her heels, and sank into the bachelor white leather sofa. A glass of fizzy white wine appeared on the coffee table, along with a bottle, its neck neatly wrapped in a napkin. "It'll be ready in a couple of minutes."

Yesenia was surprised at how comfortable the domestic routine was. She missed this part of marriage. Turning sideways and putting her legs up, she threw an arm over the back of the couch.

"How's Ryan?" she asked. His brother must have had a hand in this. Yesenia couldn't see any other way that flattened pork and sliced lemons had appeared in Cameron's place. When they were together, her mother did most of the cooking. And without Reina, Cam had subsisted on hamburgers and spaghetti from a jar.

"In love. Insufferable."

"And your mom?" She immediately regretted the question. Bridget was an argument catalyst. His response was level headed, though. "Fine," came over his shoulder. His back to her, she couldn't gauge his expression. With English being her second language, she relied heavily on reading people's faces to understand what they were really saying. "Ryan and I still have Sunday brunch with her. She needs a new fence."

Yesenia dropped her shoulders and massaged her neck. Either he'd learned to spare her the truth about what his mom thought about his plans to get back together, or Bridget had mellowed out.

"Bring the wine," Cameron said. He carried a heaping platter in one hand, and two plates in the other. She scurried to put her nearly empty glass and the bottle on the table, and came back to relieve him of the plates.

She took a place at the foot of the table. Cameron disappeared, and the lighting seemed a little dimmer when he returned, matches in hand. He lit candles, and instead of sitting six feet away at the head of the table, he took a chair right next to her.

"I don't think this is going to work," she said to the empty plate before her. She wasn't dumb. Cameron wasn't ready to sign papers of any kind, he was hell bent on seduction.

Cameron ignored her. He filled the green ceramic plate with fried pork and some kind of vegetable and rice mixture. Following his lead, she tested a few grains. It was good, surprisingly so. But she put her fork down. Yesenia didn't want to be swayed by food.

"Did you hear —"

"Loud and clear, Jessie."

"We didn't separate because we couldn't sit at a table together or sleep together. Nothing else worked."

"I never wanted the separation."

She heard her fork clang as it hit the floor, but she made no move to pick it up.

What? This was news. Wait. She *was* the news. She hated being surprised. Yesenia was used to knowing things ten hours before everyone else. Sound as loud as the waves of the Pacific pounding against the rocks in Malibu filled her ears. Her mind was a jumble, Dori's problems, hunger for food, hunger for him. None of this made sense. Her chest squeezed like she was drowning.

"I didn't go to the lawyer's office by myself. You were right there. Next to me. You agreed," she pressed.

"You thought we needed a break."

How could he be so matter-of-fact about one of the worst moments of her life? A break? This had to be a really bad joke.

Yesenia balled her hands into fists. If she tried to kill him, would he arrest her for murder? Because in a fight of her against him, he'd win. But boy would she like to give it a try right now. Sitting there now, looking smug about the possibility of reunification.

Did he forget how he'd frozen her out? What was she supposed to do? Spend the next fifty years talking to an iceberg? When he couldn't compromise on the importance of her career, her family, his job, his damned moral code, she hadn't seen any reason to stick around. Now he was talking about it like they'd broken up for a week in high school, instead of years in the real world.

She found the fork, laid it and the napkin on the table. "A break, Cameron. Our marriage was broken. I have… had…no plans to get back together." In spite of her words, that tiny flame of hope was flickering to life again, like any fire gaining momentum on its own. They had both changed so much.

"Okay," he said, lifting his knife again and sawing off first one, then another piece of pork. He chewed like he did everything, slowly, deliberately. His eyes never left hers. Cameron swallowed. A wineglass touched his full bottom lip. Golden liquid disappeared from the glass. She'd lost her appetite. Why hadn't he? Then she saw the predator he only tried to hide sometimes.

Tiny beads of sweat broke out everywhere. Like prey, her fight or flight response kicked in. She needed to get the hell out of there if she didn't want to end up in his bed. If she didn't hightail it now, she'd be ensnared like a rabbit in a trap in some grand scheme she couldn't yet work out. Yesenia put both her hands firmly on the table, gripping the edge. One push and she'd be out of there. The muscles in the back of her arms tightened. Before she could lift her butt from the chair, a single hand circled her upper arm.

"Stay."

SIX

YESENIA SWORE TO HERSELF. Cameron had always been a man of few words. When he aimed them her way, it was always devastating. She was ready to follow him anywhere, and they both knew it.

"You don't want me." She didn't know who she was trying to convince, him or her. "You don't trust me," she added. "You didn't even tell me about Ras–"

"Trust this," he said, then pulled her up and behind the gauze-thin curtain and onto the king sized bed.

Cameron didn't like criminals, wrongdoers, people who were disloyal, but no one could ever say he didn't love women. He gently eased Yesenia onto the bed and pushed up her cotton skirt. Waves of heat surrounded her face and neck.

Years ago, the first time Cameron had done this, she had been mortified. Her mother had hammered home the importance of virtue. Nice girls didn't let men touch them there. But he had. And suddenly being nice hadn't mattered a lick anymore. After that first time, there'd been no going back. Thanking God for the privacy of the apartment, she took a deep breath.

The first touch was always a shock. She sucked in another shallower breath this time.

"Some things never change, Jessie," Cameron murmured.

The pleasure that rippled through her seemed out of proportion to someone merely sliding a thumb under her panties, and through her slick folds.

He paused a very long time. Anticipation twisted her belly. Yesenia could feel her jaw slackening, breath whooshing out in puffs that seemed to stir the curtains. Time stretched. He wanted something from her. Damn. She didn't ask. He understood that. He gave. She took. That was the way it had always worked. But she sensed Cameron yearning for more.

"What do you want, Jessie?" Oh, God. Why now? Why couldn't this be the wrong thing at the right time without all the talk? Words made it real. Made them accountable. Made her accountable.

"You know," she kept her voice low.

"Tell me, Jessie."

She thanked God, she couldn't see his face. Those unblinking eyes holding her responsible. That he couldn't see the mortification that probably stained hers.

Yesenia wanted him to pull her panties off. Spread her legs. Put her knees over his shoulders. Part her with his thumbs. Paint her with his tongue.

"Touch me," she whispered in abbreviation. Cameron sighed. It wasn't enough. If she didn't give more now, he'd want more later. This new, improved Cam believed in personal responsibility.

She wasn't ready to acknowledge her part in this new relationship. Not when any future was iffy at best. Yesenia ran a hand through his hair, tracing the contours of his scalp. She opened her legs a little more, the only invitation she had the guts to offer. Because he was a man, it was an invitation he couldn't refuse.

Like a dog to a bone, Cameron came back to her, pushing her up to the headboard. She gripped the polished wood, holding on for dear life. Skimming off her underwear, he kissed the inside of each thigh. Goosebumps broke out on her skin. Then he was there. Bold strokes of his tongue bathed her in pleasure. Ripples washed over her, stronger and stronger until she stopped thinking.

The bed dipped and rolled as he kneed and elbowed his way around her body.

"Jessie. Jesus."

The scrape of wood against wood accompanied the crinkle of plastic as he folded a condom into the palm of his hand. Obviously, he didn't want to take any chances this time. A twinge of disappointment nagged at her. She mentally swatted it away.

He kissed the tops of her fingers then laid them against his chest. Any thoughts of the future evaporated. She slipped first one button, then the next from its mooring. Yesenia pulled aside the pinstripe shirt. Its blue was the exact color of Cam's eyes.

He'd never been good at picking out clothes that complimented him. For a single irrational moment she wondered if a woman had bought it for him. But before her mind had time to go down that road, he pushed her hand down to his belt. Cam had no problem asking for what he wanted. She lifted the leather from the loops of his pants. After tugging apart the snap, she eased down the zipper. A single button on powder blue boxers held his erection behind the placket.

She slipped her hand to his butt, under the waistband. Willingly he lifted his hips, and she tugged the underwear down. His penis sprang free. Hesitantly, she touched him. That part of him that brought them both so much pleasure hadn't changed.

She leaned in and kissed him squarely on his wine stained lips. He took over the kiss. It was sloppy with need, messy with want, heavenly.

He pushed her sweater and bra up under her neck. Half a day's growth of beard rasped against one breast. His fingers toyed with the nipple on the other. Reluctantly she lifted herself away from the exquisite torture for a moment. She pulled the clothes all the way off. One last time, she wanted to feel his naked body against hers.

Yesenia put her arms around him. Kissing continued right where they'd left off. He loosened his grip a little, kissing the top of her head, her neck. Cam rolled onto his back, taking her with him. She straddled him, a knee on each side. Holding him in her hand, she rubbed his cock back and forth against her clit, amazed that her belly was tightening again.

Cam fished the condom from somewhere in the bedclothes and gave it to her. "Put this on."

"I've never..." Yesenia rubbed her thumb along the

rim, trying to imagine how the latex stretched over that part.

"Not hard," he forced out between clenched teeth.

Sitting back on her haunches, she focused on tearing the foil open, squinting at the donut shaped latex. "Which side?"

But she figured it out before he answered. She rolled it down a centimeter at a time. "Just like that," Cam groaned out. She moved off him, ready to lie on her back. The way they'd always finished.

"No. Not that. Not now," he said. "Come back." He pulled her knee back over. "Stay here." Effortlessly, he spanned her waist and lifted her. "You do it."

She nearly cried with the need to be filled, the need for a second release. "I don't know what you're asking me."

Cam wrapped her hand around him, then covered it with his own. Up and down his shaft they moved. "I can't..." His hand stilled hers. "I don't want to do this alone anymore."

"You're not alone."

"Sex isn't just me fucking you, Jessie. It's us. I need it to be about both of us. I need to know you need me as much as I want you."

His language was so direct, so visceral. A nervous feeling started in her core, radiated out. She didn't know how to give him what he wanted. And she didn't have a clue what to do next.

"Put me inside."

She reached between them, feeling as awkward as a teenager. It took two tries to seat him where they both wanted him to be. Easing herself down, he filled her like he never had. She braced herself on his shoulders, her hands barely able to gain purchase on the hard cap of muscle.

They were joined like that for long minutes while she closed her eyes and reveled in the sensation. But once she opened her eyes again, the muscles of Cam's chest fascinated her. Yesenia moved once, fanning her hands through the tight blond curls, finally landing on and playing with the hard nipples there.

His hips bucked beneath her. Then Cam's hands came to her waist again. Neither of them had any choice but to move, not if they didn't want to die a slow death of anticipation. Up and down she went. It felt good, really good, but it wasn't enough.

Cam moved a hand to where they were joined. His eyes went from unfocused one moment to staring at her with laser-like intensity. Everything in her lower body tightened at the thought of what he was going to do next.

He pulled one nipple into his mouth. Released it with a pop. Then leaned in for the other. Yesenia thought she would die right there. But this wasn't an elevator or even an earthquake. Death wasn't around the corner. This was life in all its blissful glory. Cam eased her back upright, and they started their rhythm again. Like an old watch, her body wound tight again. He pushed her knees apart, capturing the most sensitive part of her between his thumbs. One squeeze, two, and she nearly rocketed off him. But he caught her, pumping into her until his climax left him bare. It was the most vulnerable she ever saw him. Without armor or artifice, there was the man she'd fallen in love with those many years before.

If she could see him this clearly, he could probably see through her as well. She turned away, not wanting to have a single soul-bearing exchange. The bed dipped. He went away briefly. A toilet flushed. Water ran. Yesenia was lifting her comforter, ready to hide when Cam came back, wineglass and bottle in hand.

"Jessie."

Her name was a command. She peeled back the covers.

He filled the glass, tipping it to her lips first, then to his.

"For our entire marriage, you were the good girl. I was the bad boy corrupting you with sex. I think we needed a more equal partnership," Cam said, setting the empty stemware on the bedside table.

Had he strung together three sentences? What did he mean by equal partnership? Why was she even considering it? He had to understand.

"I'm a good girl, Cameron."

"Got that. Now what?"

"I was supposed to be a virgin on my wedding night. Modesty above all else, Mama always said."

Explaining Catholic girl guilt to someone raised without religion was too hard. Yesenia shook her head. Having sex in the dark was one thing. Talking about it was another. Marriage had been a refuge. The majority of their sex life had been within church-sanctioned holy matrimony. It was silly to someone like him. But marriage had made her comfortable enough to make love with him anytime he asked. To enjoy it. Have orgasms. Not feel too guilty about using birth control. But the other stuff. The partnership. Her taking the lead. That was asking too much.

"I can't talk about this right now," she finally said.

He sat up and snapped on the bedside light. Pulled small glasses from a pouch on the table.

"You need reading glasses?" He looked so defenseless in the tiny spectacles. She let a little laugh escape.

"Get the papers. I need to see where to sign."

Her mirth dried up in an instant. "I'm not buying the condo."

"Seriously?" He pulled off the glasses and lay them back down on the table. His stare was unforgiving.

"I can't make the down payment or pay closing costs."

"What happened to the money?"

"I have to hire a lawyer for Dori."

♥

CAMERON POURED himself another glass of wine. Guzzled it like it was a beer and he was at a fraternity hazing ritual.

He emptied the remains from the bottle into the wineglass. Sipped this time. Liquid in his mouth made it impossible to yell at Jessie. Ryan had said to him more than once when they made the list that family acceptance would go a long way toward healing their marriage. But God damn it. Did acceptance mean he had to stand by and watch while they were taking advantage of her? She wanted one thing for herself and if Reina and Dolores had their way, she wasn't going to be able to have it.

"Did Dori ask you to do that?"

"No, she told Mama that she was going to get it from Raul."

"Why didn't you let her?"

"You know Raul. You've arrested him. He wouldn't give my sister money without extracting some kind of payment. I don't want her selling herself on the street or risk being a drug mule or something like that."

"I wouldn't ever let it come to that."

"You think I'm an idiot for giving the money to a lawyer, right?"

Cameron picked through that minefield and chose his words carefully. "I think you're a loving sister."

"Who got suckered in by her mama and sister again."

"I didn't say that."

"But I know you think it."

"I'm not going to let you pick a fight with me, Jessie."

"I came here to ask you for help with Dori."

The truth, so starkly said, was a blow. Even though deep down, he'd known she hadn't come because of him, but in spite of him. He'd thought it was because he was standing in the way of her owning the condo. Instead it was her family. Hardening his resolve, he took in more wine.

"What can I do for you?"

Jessie looked ready to fall off the bed. Took a good five seconds before she closed her mouth. "I...what..."

"I can lend you money to buy the condo. It's important to you." Living frugally for the last couple of years had given him a nice-sized savings account. Money he was more than willing to spend on Jessie.

"I wouldn't take your money." Jessie hesitated a long time. "But—"

"Spit it out."

"You know what. It's nothing, Cam. I'll take care of this myself. The best I can."

He didn't know whether to be disappointed because she hadn't asked for something he couldn't give without compromising his principles, or relieved.

"You're not going to ask me to dismiss the charges?"

"It's not like I didn't consider it. But you've never done a favor for anyone ever, Cameron Becker. You are the most honest, upstanding, loyal, fair, play-no-favorites LAPD officer ever."

He was confused more than ever. Isn't loyal, fair, and upstanding what a city wanted in an employee, a woman wanted in a man? "You say that like it's a crime."

"In our case, Cameron, it's always been a bad thing. You have greater loyalty to the force than your family. You love something that can't love you back."

Like that, he pushed away his vow not to fight. "You're being unfair, Yesenia."

"How?"

"I may not have let Dori out of jail. I couldn't do that without jeopardizing my job. Maybe another officer could get away with it. But I'm under greater scrutiny at the force."

"I can't apologize any more for my stupidity, Cameron."

"I'm not asking you to. I'm asking you to understand why I have to go by the book."

"I understand. I'm just…I guess I'm just unhappy with

the whole situation. You can't help Dori. I can't help her either."

He watched Jessie stand, snap on her bra, and pull on her panties, followed by the rest of her clothes. Cam stared at the empty wineglass in his hands. This was not how it was supposed to go. He had planned to give her what she wanted, freedom and her own place, woo her with wine, food, and well…the magic in his pants. Forge a new future together. Instead they were at the same old crossroads again. His job and her family squarely between them. Their marriage was like gridlock. And like L.A. traffic, he couldn't see a way out of it.

"You're leaving?" he asked. He'd hoped she would stay and that they could figure out a way back to each other. But the time was never right for them.

"I have to go home. Get some sleep. Figure out how I'm going to get my sister out of this mess. If she's deported, Mama will kill me."

SEVEN

YESENIA WAS damp and hot by the time she found parking on Wilshire Boulevard. She stuffed as many quarters as she could find on the Jeep's floor into a meter. Retrieving her car held ransom in a tow lot was not on her list of things to do before broadcast. A ticket would be the worst thing that could happen to her today. She wished she could say the same for Dori.

She glanced at the business card, then sized up the buildings rising from the pavement. Ignoring the sweat trickling between her breasts, she sighed in relief. Dolores' appointment was in a squat four story structure, next to a fifteen story monstrosity next door. Smiling for the security guard who recognized her got Yesenia stair access with no questions asked.

"Sorry I'm late," she said, barging into the office that held her sister and the lawyer she'd hired on Ernesto's recommendation.

Dolores was leaning forward, full cleavage on display from the low cut top. The handsome young lawyer stood behind a desk bigger than him. The attorney was flustered, having been caught taking in the view.

"Victor Alvarado."

He wasn't the first man, nor probably the last, to be bowled over by her sister's charms. Out of her usual velour sweats, Dolores was in skin tight seven hundred dollar jeans, no doubt courtesy of Raul, leather boots, and a white lace top that managed to be conservative and sexy at the same time. For a brief moment, Yesenia envied her sister's flair. Dori probably wouldn't have a problem with a give and take relationship in the bedroom.

Comparing herself with Dori was inevitable. How could she not? She had citizenship, a career, and even a husband, though estranged. Dori had none of that. So she had to rely on what she could: wits, looks, Raul. She cleared her head and sat in the empty chair, leaned forward and extended her hand. "How are you related to Jose Alvarado?"

"I'm one of his sons," he said, grasping her fingers and shaking.

A son. For the kind of money she had, she didn't rate the lawyer who regularly had lunch with the local ad guys at KESP.

"So you're saying it isn't true?" Dolores asked.

"What isn't true?" Yesenia interjected. Since she was paying, she at least needed to know what was going on here.

Dolores turned to her. "You remember how Mama said that Julia got pulled over for a traffic ticket? Next thing she knew, Julia had gotten a green card. Same thing for Raul's cousin in Georgia. He got busted for driving without a license. The judge took pity on him. Got him a green card. Maybe this arrest could be serendipity, was all I was saying."

It took Yesenia a moment to grasp the meaning of Dolores' last sentence.

"Habla español?" Yesenia asked the lawyer out of courtesy, and then asked her sister in Spanish what she meant.

"Wait," the lawyer said. Yesenia stopped talking to Dori to look at him. *"Solamente un poquito,"* he said.

Great. She'd assumed all immigration lawyers in Los Angeles spoke Spanish. They'd all be on better footing if the conversation were in her native language. It would guarantee no misunderstandings. If she weren't paying by the hour, having paid well into this one, she'd have asked for a reassignment. But Dori was there. Anything Yesenia didn't understand, Dori could explain later. She looked at the *abogado*. An immigration lawyer who didn't speak Spanish. That was rich. If she wasn't so annoyed, she'd almost have felt sorry for him.

"Fine, English then," she said curtly. Yesenia couldn't afford to spend her savings on chit-chat. She had to get back to her paying job. Money had to come in before it could go out. "Bottom line, what are Dolores' options?"

Alvarado's nice guy demeanor disappeared and he was all business. Good. "She can plead guilty. Petition for a moral turpitude waiver."

She glared at her sister. Dolores had said it was marijuana, not prostitution. She'd been stupid to ignore Cameron's well-sourced information. "Moral turpitude?"

A look passed between the lawyer and her sister. "Drug possession is considered immoral by the ICE. They don't honor California's medical marijuana laws," Alvarado said.

"Dori, I told you that a thousand times. But you insisted you needed it for your anxiety." Yesenia all but said out loud that she didn't believe even a little bit that her sister had any kind of condition that required the liberal application of marijuana.

"A doctor gave me my card," Dori retorted.

"The *doctor* you found on Venice beach could be bought for forty dollars." She looked toward Alvarado who probably thought her family was crazy. "Sorry. About this possible waiver?"

"Possession of less than thirty grams, and the U.S. government may not count it against an undocumented person when they apply for a change in status."

For the first time in days, Yesenia's heart beat at a normal rhythm. "That's a relief. Now can we talk about what you were doing there with Raul? How many times does he have to get you in trouble?"

Alvarado looked from Yesenia to Dori and back again. "Even though you're paying the bills, Yesenia, what Dolores tells me remains confidential. She decides how much to share with you." To Dolores, he said, "Do you want to continue this without your sister?"

Dori nodded. Yesenia couldn't believe it. Her sister had nodded her out of the room. If Yesenia hadn't had a full day ahead and wasn't on probation in her new anchor spot, she would have put up a fight. She got up slowly and walked to the door, her brain whirring. Resisting the urge to slam it, she closed the door softly behind her. All the tough love experts she'd read over the years would probably say it wasn't her battle anyway. Would this non Spanish-speaking guy be able to save Dori from deportation?

She tried to use the run down the stairs as an opportunity to relieve some of the tension in her body. It didn't work. The thought of Dori on a prison bus to dusty Tijuana filled her head. The chaos of the newsroom and the oblivion of joining the nightly infotainment broadcast held greater appeal than ever.

The thought of Dori in Mexico worried her down the stairs, in the car, and out on location. It bothered her through interviews with solid citizens about the pending arrest of their district councilman, and the opening of a much needed grocery in Pacoima.

She flubbed twice during her stand up in the field. The camera guy, pounds of heavy camera on his shoulder and loaded down with more weight from battery on his belt, gave her the evil eye.

"You're usually more professional, Yesenia. Anchor desk making your head big already?"

"No. I know my job. I won't mess up again," she said firmly, shoving all thoughts of Dori and deportation from her head. The last thing she needed were any hint of rumors that she was hard to work with, getting back to Ernesto. If she didn't keep this job and turn her probationary period as weeknight anchor into something more permanent—there'd be no money for the mortgage on Mama's house, or lawyers, or much of anything else.

She made it through the rest of the day and the broadcast without a single blunder. At her desk after sign-off, she finally had a chance to call Dori. Even though it was rounding midnight when she finally got home, Yesenia didn't hesitate a moment to pick up the phone.

"What's the bottom line?" she asked without preamble.

"Moral turpitude applies to more than prostitution," Dori said.

"I heard the lawyer. I don't care what you got charged with, Dori. So we'll pretend you didn't sell yourself on Sunset Boulevard."

"The U.S. considers drug possession immoral."

"As do I. So on that, I and the U.S. Congress agree. But I'm not having a political discussion with you. Or talking about *putas*. Can you get the waiver? Is there a way to get you off so we don't have to think about petitioning for anything?"

"*If* I have to plead guilty and get a waiver, I can still apply for permanent residency without this affecting me. But that's a lot of 'ifs'."

Yesenia didn't hear the rest as she nearly fell down with relief. Dori hadn't messed up completely. A green card may be as far out on the horizon as the setting sun over Santa Monica Pier, but it was out there. Doing rough calculations in her head, she figured if she sold the new Jeep, gave up the apartment before it was sold out under her, and moved back home, she could save enough to hire a real lawyer this time, jump the hurdle of their illegal entry, and finally get her family citizenship. For a long moment she cursed the mistakes she'd made. Hiring a paralegal when she first got out of school. He'd taken ten thousand dollars and gotten them no closer to citizenship. Finally getting her citizenship after marrying Cameron, and failing to do more for her family before 9/11.

She didn't share any of this with her sister, though. She'd have to raise the money, and present it to her family as a done deal. Admonishing Dori to stay out of trouble, she hung up the phone. She was elated that Dori's latest mistake hadn't been fatal either to her in body, or to her chances of remaining in the U.S. Maybe it would work like Mama's folk tales. Getting in trouble might get her citizenship.

That elation quickly changed to defeat. Her one opportunity at freedom and independence was gone. It would be a long time before it came around again. She tried not to look around her apartment with longing. She'd loved finally living on her own, without having to watch Dori piss her life away, and without her mother's constant nagging. And this time she hadn't had to be married to do it. Maybe she and Cam could have worked out. She didn't know. Might never know. But she had run into her marriage looking for shelter. The next time she got married she wanted to run toward love and fulfillment, not away from her family and responsibility.

The Jeep, the apartment with only her name on the title, those markers of success would have to wait. Why did she need a house and car anyway? Los Angeles was a city of renters and leasers. She could appear to have it all for half the price. Whatever. She needed to get to bed so she didn't come to work with suitcase-sized bags under her eyes. Yesenia was able to sleep peacefully, secure in the knowledge that at least she wouldn't have to pack her sister's bags first thing in the morning.

EIGHT

YESENIA LOOKED AT THE CLOCK. Six AM and the phone was already ringing. Cameron worked her same shift, so the likely culprit was Mama. With some fondness, she remembered the days when she and Dori had conspired to lace Mama's *horchata* with sleeping pills on more than one Saturday night.

But it was Wednesday, not Sunday, and she had to get up anyway. So she picked up on Mama's second try, not doing the usual muting of the ringer until the voice mail button went from slow blink to solid red.

"You need to come over, now," Mama screeched into the phone.

"Is it Dolores?" She feared those few precious hours were the last sleep she was going to get for a long while.

"Yes. She says she's going back to Mexico!"

Yesenia took a deep breath. This decision was completely out of the blue. Not six hours ago, she'd thought her sister was going to stay and fight. But how could she have expected that? Fighting was not Dori's way. In that way the Morales girls were complete opposites.

She'd fought her way out of agoraphobia, anxiety, and undocumented status. While Dori had let her and Mama guide her life. Let Raul steer her off the tracks.

"Are you there, Yesenia? What are we going to do? She wants me to come with her."

She promised to come over. After a quick shower, Yesenia stuffed her work clothes into her portable garment bag. She decided to take the tongue lashing her mother was going to give when she showed up in sweats. But it was too damned early, and this was too damned important to wait until she was in full battle armor.

Twenty-four minutes later, she stood at the front door of her mother's house. The iron bars of the security door were cool and damp. She held on tight for a long time, seeking to ground herself. Screwing up her courage against the fear of what was to come, she stepped into the house.

Silence greeted her instead of yelling. Mama was bustling in the kitchen. Dori was tapping away at the iPad. And Raul, remote control in hand, was flipping from one brightly colored morning show to the next.

She started with the easiest target first. "Raul, how is it you're out of jail?"

"Never got arrested."

"You threw Dori under the bus to save your skinny ass?"

"She asked to work for me. Told her this shit was dangerous. But your sister did what she wanted."

Yesenia wasn't so sure of that. "You think she should go to Mexico?"

"Nah, man. I can't even remember Mexico. She doesn't either. Don't know how anyone can live without creature comforts."

"Dolores?" She looked at her sister. There were two things she noticed. First, her sister's back was rigid, upright. She was working on the tablet with a sense of purpose. Second, she wasn't high.

"I don't know why Mama called you. I'm an adult, old enough to make a decision. And this is the one I'm making."

"I called her because you've gone crazy. We left that godforsaken place for a reason."

Here we go again. Yesenia was that reason. She braced herself for the speech. It didn't come.

"Mama, if we only left for Yesenia, then she's fine. She's got her papers, she's working. She's even got a husband if she chooses."

"But the news says Mexico's crazy. We're going to be shot by blood thirsty warlords."

"Cool the drama."

"Why do you want Mama to go with you?" Yesenia stemmed the tide of guilt that threatened to close her throat. She loved Mama, dearly. A little distance between them wouldn't be a bad thing. Solutions to her biggest life challenges lay within reach. Did it have to come from such a tragic situation, though? When she got no answer, she moved on to practical matter. "How would you even do this?"

"Aren't you going to talk her out of this? Aren't you going to get that lawyer to do something? Can't you get your husband to pull a few strings?"

She looked her mother square in the eye. "Don't you think Cameron's done enough for this family?"

Mama couldn't meet her eye. A big sheet of plastic was the sole barrier between them as Mama wrapped a tray of some kind of food.

"Mama?"

"I don't know anyone there anymore. It's been years, decades. I only know about life here in America now."

Yesenia turned back to Dori. "You have a plan?"

"My cousin can get her a job." Raul said.

She spun on him. He was the reason Dori was in this trouble in the first damned place.

"What, as a drug mule? Is she supposed to stuff drugs up her *coño* and hide in the trunks of cars? We've already seen what kind of jobs you have for my sister."

Raul held out his hands in supplication. Should have practiced that move in church more often. Maybe he wouldn't be the degenerate he was today. "I'm serious. My cousin works at a call center in Mexico City. He said the guy in Encino is always hiring. He says —"

"The one who was deported? The one who doesn't speak a lick of Spanish?"

"Yes." Raul's voice was more serious than she'd ever heard it. All the laid back Bill & Ted was gone. Contrition was a temporary cure for asshole.

"Give me his number."

"Who?"

"Your damned contact in Encino, that's who. Throw in your cousin's number for good measure."

Dori found a pad and paper and Yesenia took the information down. She turned to leave.

"Where are you going?" Mama called.

"To make some calls. I have to get to work."

Out the front door, the first call she made was to Cameron.

"Are you working today?" She hoped upon hope he hadn't switched to the morning shift. "Can you meet me?"

❦

CAMERON PULLED another button-down shirt from his closet. Jessie hadn't sounded like she was in a t-shirt and jeans mood when she'd called.

Uncharacteristically, his wife was sitting on the front steps looking like someone had kicked her in the gut.

"What are you doing outside?"

She didn't answer. Jessie pulled her head from one shoulder to another. "I took the day off work."

He stayed where he was, a good ten paces from her. She'd never taken a day off work that he could remember.

"Dori wants to take a voluntary departure."

Cameron's head spun as he tried to wrap his brain around what she was saying. "She wants to go back to Mexico?"

"Yes. And take Mama with her."

Minefield. Even without a metal detector, Cameron knew one when he saw it. He did what he did best, stayed silent.

A purple Post-it note fluttered on her finger as she waved the paper around. "I need to see Victor Alvarado and then this guy."

He tried not to shift his weight or seem impatient. A man needed mind reading skills with a woman. His were on vacation.

"Will you go with me now?"

"I'll drive," he said, tossing his keys in the air. That much he could do.

Once they were in the car, Jessie got on the phone and got the lawyer's schedule cleared.

He pulled into a space on a side street, came around and helped her out of the car.

"Elevator?"

"Only four stories," she said and they walked the quarter mile to the building. In the third floor lobby, she turned to him. "He doesn't speak Spanish."

He knew that was a slight of the highest order. Jessie thought every Mexican in the U.S., if not most Angelenos should speak both languages. He almost felt sorry for the guy.

Victor looked wary when they entered. Cam patted himself down. Nope, he didn't have a gun. Squirrely guy. Wondered how this one got picked, but decided not to ask. He must have some redeeming value beyond a law license.

They sat in his office. Victor closed the door before returning to his high backed leather chair. Someone should have told the lawyer the oversized seat made him look like a kid playing dress up.

"You know I can't discuss the details of your sister's case. Confidentiality reasons."

"I'm not here as a family member. I'm here as a reporter for KESP." Jessie set a mini tape recorder on the desk. Clicked it on. "Hypothetical case. Undocumented Mexican gets arrested for a couple of misdemeanors. What are her options?"

Heaving a sigh, Alvarado slumped. "She'd probably have three options." Good, the man knew on which side his bread was buttered. Not only was Jessie paying the bill, but she had the megaphone of television. "Fight the charges. But doing that may bring her to the attention of the ICE. She could be found guilty or plead guilty. But then she'd serve a jail term and face immigration detention and ultimately deportation."

"What's the third option?"

"If she wasn't under threat from her government or drug lords, then I might advise her to take herself home."

"Could she ever come back?"

"Maybe. Only a handful of voluntary departure applicants get background checks. So she could go, and possibly apply for entry at a later date."

"But there's no prohibition for her to travel to the U.S., right?"

"Probably not. But I would encourage the family legally residing in the U.S. to visit their relatives in Mexico."

"Oh." The indignation and fight had left Jessie in an instant.

She poked around the edges looking for a solution, but

didn't find much of anything to deal with the fundamental issue — Dolores had screwed up big time.

Cam followed her directions and drove them from the business corridor of the Wilshire District to a nearly carbon copy area on the border of Sherman Oaks and Encino.

The mysterious Alejandro of the purple Post-it was on the fifteenth floor of the building. He took a deep breath ready to tackle the climb. Jessie had gotten him in the habit of taking the steps and he'd never really shook it.

But the guard refused stair access.

"I'm here," he said. "Can you do it?"

"Can you hold my hand?"

He gripped it hard, pressing the up button. The elevator was empty when they stepped on. Using his other hand, he kept the door open while she made the move onto the carpeted floor of the car.

"Press fifteen."

Jessie gripped his hand with ferocity and held her breath at the same time. When a ding sounded and the doors opened, she got out like the hounds of hell were on her heels.

A big logo greeted them in the corridor. The gleaming hub and spoke wheel affixed to the wall said nothing about what the company did.

Jessie took a moment to shake off her fear and turned toward the huge reception desk on the right. "I'm here for Alejandro Molinero."

A guy not five minutes over eighteen greeted them. Cameron shook his hand, scanning his fully tattooed arm for gang symbols. Nothing there. A bunch of trees and buildings, but nothing else. Cameron made a big effort not to shake his head. When did it become okay to wear earrings and tattoos to your day job? Country was going to hell in a handbasket. And Jessie wanted her family to stay? Maybe they had some semblance of order in Mexico.

"How can I help you?" Alejandro said.

"Can we go back to your office?" Jessie asked.

For a moment, the kid looked embarrassed. "There's no office. And there's head honchos meeting in the conference room." He gestured to the guest chairs lined up like fence pickets. "We can talk here."

"Your friend Raul knows my sister."

Alejandro immediately looked wary. Apparently Raul's drug dealing, pimping reputation was widely known. "Yeah."

"Did he call you about getting my job a sister in Mexico?"

"Dolores?"

"She's my sister."

"Um. Okay. Well, I can get her an interview here for a job in our Mexico City call center."

"Paying what?"

"Compensation is —"

"Confidential, I'm sure," Jessie said. She pulled her press credentials from her bag. "I'm not here in an official capacity. I just want to know what my sister's getting into. If you know Raul, you know I can't trust him."

"Pays about five dollars U.S. an hour. The minimum wage is only five dollars a day there. So we're competitive.

Our employees enjoy a middle class lifestyle in Mexico similar to what they have here."

"We don't need the PR spiel," Cameron couldn't help saying.

Alejandro eyed him. "Gotcha, Officer."

Everyone assumed he was a god damn cop even without flashing the badge. While he was wondering if that was a good or bad thing, Jessie was finishing up with Alejandro.

The ride down the elevator probably left as many bruises on his right hand as the earlier ride had made on his left.

When they got in the car, she turned to him. "What do you think?"

"About?"

"Should I let her go?"

"Don't think you have much choice."

"Why?"

"She's an adult, Jessie. Dori got into trouble and is making the best of the situation. You should be proud of her for getting out ahead of this."

"I can't fix it, can I?"

"Maybe Dolores *is* fixing it. I met you because I arrested Raul. Back then it was petty theft and low level dealing. That's escalated. Informants say that he's moved up the chain for drugs, and has moved into bringing girls across the border for sex work. Dolores has never been able to quit him. This will finally force her to do what I told her to do at the police station that first time."

Jessie pulled his hand from the gearshift. She squeezed, not as hard as earlier. Hope leapt into his chest.

She was touching him out of honest affection, not from fear or desperation.

"Thank you for coming with me today. I needed to find out for myself."

"That's what husbands are for. We're in this together, you know. We always have been."

She let go of his hand and smiled at him before turning and staring out at the traffic from the window.

For once he was grateful the traffic was slow. "You ready to go home?"

"Yeah, I think so. Maybe I'll just veg and think."

He walked her to the front door.

She hesitated, blushed. "You want to come in?"

Cameron's dick jumped to half mast. His wife wanted to have sex with him. His heart skipped a little happy dance inside his chest. It was working. "I think I'm going to head on home," he heard himself say, restraint keeping him in check for once.

Jessie shifted, looking like she wanted to hug him, kiss him, maybe shake his hand. He couldn't tell. "So, I guess I'll see you."

Cameron got a little closer. Kissed her on the forehead. Inhaled that smell so uniquely hers. He should pull away now, but he couldn't. He kissed both her eyelids, her cheeks. The heart that beat against his chest thumped a little faster. Breath panted in his ear. Because he couldn't resist, he took her lips. Brushing against them slowly, keeping it chaste. "I want you to call me. Anytime."

She thrust a thumb toward the front door. "Are you sure you don't want...some of Mama's cooking?"

"I didn't come here for food, or sex. I came because

your family's going through a hard time and you needed me. That's what couples do for each other. Think on that tonight while you're thinking about Reina and Dolores."

Before the little head could change the big head's mind, he lifted her right hand, kissed it. Turning on his heel, he strode to the car.

NINE

A WEEK later Cameron looked at the phone buzzing in his hand. No one who valued their life called him this early in the morning. The 323 number was vaguely familiar, but he couldn't place it when he swiped to accept the call.

"Yeah."

"It's Reina Prado, Yesenia's mama," she said. Like he wouldn't recognize that voice.

"Of course, Reina. How can I help you?" Cameron was wary. Reina had been nice to him when he proposed to Jessie, making an honest woman of her, when he helped Jessie get citizenship, when he helped them buy the house. But when the INS closed the door on possible citizenship for her and Dolores, he had become the bad guy. They had all entered the country without visas and there was little he could do to change that. But Reina didn't see it that way. Somehow he'd become the embodiment of much that was wrong. As if he could wave his LAPD badge and make it all better.

He resisted the urge to disconnect the call. He'd vowed to be there for Jessie and a huge part of that was accepting her family for how they were, even if that was needy and angry.

"I'm having some people over for breakfast. I want you to come."

"Okay, I'll call Jessie and pick her up on the way," he said.

"No. Jessie's already coming. I want you here."

He made a mental note of the time he was to be over the next morning and disconnected the call.

He pulled up behind Jessie's white Jeep at the appointed hour. In response to her raised eyebrow, he said, "Your mom called. Said it was important."

For a long moment, she stood there, obviously at a loss. He gave into the urge tugging him forward, and pulled her into a tight embrace. She relaxed into him. They held each other for a long second. It was like a time machine pulling them back to the years when all they'd needed was each other before work and family got in the way.

"We should go in," he whispered through her hair. If he wanted to get on even footing with Jessie's family, he didn't want to be late.

Following Jessie through first the iron, then the wood door, he was engulfed in a hug from Reina. Dolores' welcome was effusive as well. He looked around to make sure he was in the right place. He could count the times Reina had hugged him on a single hand. Maybe it wasn't a time machine, but a personality transplant machine that had fucked with the space time continuum. Reina wasn't exactly a social butterfly, more like a curtain-flicking nosy neighbor. Nonetheless, their house looked like New Year's, Christmas, and Cinco de Mayo all wrapped up in one. Except it was nine o'clock on a Wednesday morning, one of the least celebratory days of the week by his reckoning.

In response to Jessie's eyebrows, even closer to her hairline now, he gave a tiny shrug. No one had clued him in. Maybe Dolores was getting married or was pregnant, though he couldn't imagine Reina pouring out little shots of strong Mexican coffee, and passing *sopes* if Dori was knocked up with Raul's baby.

Staying in the country, tied up with Raul, who was hellbent on living life on the wrong side of the law had to be the worst of all possible decisions. He took the plateful of food handed him by a man about Reina's age, and sat down at the last free dining room chair.

"Mama, what's going on?" Jessie finally asked. She remained standing, stiff as a board, her purse clutched in a tight fingered grip, her back against the wall.

"We're moving," Reina said, joviality personified.

He soaked in the personality transplant. Was this the woman who just last week was bemoaning the fact that Dolores wanted to go back to a country plagued with drug cartel violence? Jessie was not jovial. Her face was taut with distress. He'd thought after their talks with the lawyer and the outsourcing guy, she'd made peace with her sister's decision.

Obviously not. Cameron pushed away his plate. Put his knife and fork down. Despite the mouthwatering smells wafting up from the food, this was a meal he wasn't going to be able to enjoy.

"*¿Dónde, Mamá?*" Jessie's voice was full of resignation. She'd roll with whatever they said, he knew. She'd sacrifice whatever she had to.

"Mexico City," Reina said, clapping her hands together like a toddler taking her first steps.

A loud chorus of cheers in Spanish arose from everyone around the table. China coffee cups clinked together.

"Mama? Dolores?" Jessie's voice rose above the din. "There's still a chance Dolores could win this case, be found innocent."

"I'll still be on the ICE radar. I can't wait for the hammer of deportation to drop. How many times have you told me to take charge of my life? I am. Not you. Not Raul."

"Mama? You always said you were grateful to be out of Mexico."

"Dolores promised me I don't have to work if I don't want to. I miss my family."

"You never said anything about that," Jessie said.

"You weren't the only person making a sacrifice, Yesenia." To Dolores, Reina said, "*Dígaselo a tu hermana.*"

Yesenia pulled Dolores to the corner. Abandoning a perfectly good breakfast once and for all, he followed his wife's pleading eyes. She needed backup. When he joined them, Jessie's hand was tight upon her sister's wrist, tugging insistently.

"I'm tired, sis. I know it may not seem like it, but I'm tired of not being able to work, worrying every time I drive a car or cross in the middle of the street. Nearly shitting my pants every time I pass the federal building, or drive to San Diego. I want to go home."

"Mexico isn't home. None of us have been there in over twenty years. It's not some resort. It's a gang infested hell hole."

"Does that mean you won't visit?" Dolores said, a sad smile tilting her lips.

Jessie's hands moved further up her sister's slim arms. She shook Dolores, hard. "This is not funny."

For the first time in a long time, Cameron saw Dolores' face firm with determination. Gone was the lackadaisical weed haze she usually wore. Jessie's sister was serious and probably unshakeable. "I already have a job, Yesenia," she said.

Jessie looked as surprised as he was. Dolores had never held a job. Not a real job. He remembered her working under the table at some restaurant, helping her mom with cleaning jobs, even picking up the occasional childcare work. None had lasted longer than it took to earn enough for some designer jeans or a fancy phone Jessie wouldn't buy. He'd always thought Dolores was allergic to work.

"You take that call center job?"

"Alejandro said you and Cam showed up at their office. So you know it's legit. I went in. He interviewed me. Offered me a job. Maybe that college degree you made me get is actually worth something."

Jessie ignored the dig.

"Where are you going to live?"

"SOB Solutions set us up with temporary housing.

Mama can look for a permanent place down there while I'm working."

"Dolores —"

"I want to stop running, Yesenia. I want to live."

"What about this place?" Cameron hadn't heard one word about the house Jessie'd sacrificed to buy for them.

"Cameron, can you help her with the stuff we don't take?" Dolores asked, acknowledging him.

He wanted to scold Dolores for leaving L.A. without a thought for her sister, but nodded instead. He and Jessie could handle it.

"But —" Jessie was at a loss for words.

"But what? We won't bother you anymore. Do you think I wanted to spend the rest of my life relying on my sister *por dinero, por abogados, todo?*"

"I never complained." To them, Cameron thought. She'd complained mightily and bitterly to him over the years. And when he agreed that they were taking advantage, somehow *he* was in the wrong.

"You didn't have to. Let this guy make you happy. That's all he's ever wanted," Dolores said.

Jessie's sister walked back to the celebratory group. Cameron shoved open the back door and urged her outside. They'd handed his wife over to him. He wasn't going to waste the opportunity.

TEN

AIR. She needed air. After pushing her way out the back door, Yesenia took great gasping gulps of freeway-tinged, particulate-heavy, smog brown air. For once she was grateful for the ever present hum of L.A. traffic. The noise of the Santa Monica freeway drowned out her thoughts. The slam of the back door brought her back.

Move. To Mexico? Doing the one thing they'd all be avoiding her whole life? Why hadn't she taken Dori seriously in the lawyer's office? Why hadn't she pushed the LAPD harder to dismiss the charges? She hadn't wanted to put Cam into an awkward position. But she could have asked Rivera. She'd known Cam's partner nearly as long as she'd known him. Yesenia shook her head of all the regrets and recriminations. It was all water under the bridge.

Her family's plans made no sense. And made perfect sense. Some guru KESP had interviewed when she'd subbed on the morning show talked about walking into fear. Was that what Dori was doing?

"Do you want to get breakfast?" Cam asked. She'd forgotten he was there. He must have been the cause of the door slam. But there he was, looking like a rock. She needed something strong, hard, and stable right now as the sandy California soil shifted under her feet.

She turned to him. "Roscoe's?"

He nodded. "See you in five."

Nearly every fight they'd ever had involved making up at L.A.'s iconic chicken and waffles stand. They'd order food then ask the waitress for a doggy bag not five seconds after she dropped the meal. After their blowouts, they hadn't really been so much hungry for food as for each other. Greasy bags in hand, they'd drive to their little rented house on Formosa and devour each other. Thankfully, the mile drive from her mother's house didn't allow Yesenia to fall too deeply into memories of the past. The last time they'd been there, they'd had neither the food nor each other.

Emptying her mind, she focused on squeezing into the tight lot next to Cam's car. At least she didn't have to worry about marring the perfection of the pearl white paint. There would be no more lawyers. She wouldn't have to choose between her family and herself. She slammed the door, leaning against it. She could keep the car. It was all done.

Pulling off her sunglasses, she walked into the squat single-story restaurant. The darkness enveloped her like a shroud. With its scarred wood booths, it wasn't the kind of place that renovated every year, chasing the latest trends. Its caché was in being exactly what you remembered it to be.

Cam waved her over to a table. A half cup of lemonade accompanied a half glass of water on her side of the table. Was there nothing he forgot? She sat, and poured the water into the lemonade, taking some of the sting from the sugary sweet concoction.

"Got you a number thirteen, Carol B. Special," he said. It was exactly what she wanted, a fried chicken breast and waffle. For once, she forgave his chauvinism. "You going to be okay?" he asked.

Yesenia promptly forgot about fights, sex, and waffles past. Dolores' resolve and determination came rushing back at her. "So many years, we've been out of Mexico."

"Your sister's finally taking responsibility," Cam said.

"She's being stupid. Who makes a decision to move—to another country—in a week?" She saw a couple of patrons look their way. Slipping her sunglasses back down, she continued in a quieter voice. "You seem so accepting even though you've always been one of Dori's harshest critics. If she was moving to Arizona or some-thing, *you'd* say she was being stupid."

"Arizona *would* be a bad idea."

"She could get killed in Mexico."

"I'm pretty sure your sister won't get in the middle of a drug war," Cam said, his voice all calm rationality.

She wanted to yell. Get him to see her side of things. But the arrival of breakfast curtailed discussion for a moment.

"If your sister got a green card and took a job in New York City would you be upset?" he asked.

"No, of course not." She wanted Dori close. To keep an eye on her. But she would certainly understand her sister following a great job opportunity. Yesenia picked up her utensils and started in on the work of making bite sized pieces of breast.

"This isn't much different," he said. She drew in a sharp breath then sawed into her meat with renewed vigor. A major life decision and they hadn't even consulted her, not really. Not in any meaningful way that counted.

"How long is the flight?" he asked.

"Too long." She took a single bite. Not her mama's food, but it was good. She took a second bite, of waffle this time. When she'd first spied this place as a teenager she couldn't figure out this bizarre American combination. She knew what chicken was. But waffles were something you got in a yellow box from the supermarket. The two foods together, though, were great. It was one of the many things she'd misjudged about this country.

"Three, maybe four hours, Jessie," Cam said, interrupting her trip down memory lane. "That's less than New York.

In through her nose, out through her mouth the air traveled. Despite the deep breathing, her eyes smarted, and the trickle of tears rolled down her cheeks. She pushed her glasses up again, grabbed a stiff paper napkin and dabbed at the wetness leaking out. Great, now she could go on air looking like a bloated fish. She turned her head away from Cam and the other diners, toward the window.

He abandoned his food and came to sit beside her. One thick arm slipped behind her waist, pulling her to him. The other gripped the hand she'd filled with shredded, damp napkin.

For a long moment she was rigid, fighting against him. Fighting against it all. Suddenly, she relaxed, all the fight going out of her, letting her back curve into him. Slackening her muscles, she folded against her ex-husband. Letting the solid, loyal, no-nonsense man she'd avoided, hold her.

"I feel so horrible," she whispered.

The world narrowed to no one but him and her. "Why?"

"Because part of me is relieved. That I don't have to try to fix it all, the money problem, Raul and Dolores, their papers." She held the sob down as long as she could. It burst out with a laugh and a hiccough.

"The other part."

"Will miss them terribly. They're not perfect. But they've been all I've had in America."

"You have me."

Yesenia's heart raced. She wanted to believe that. Believe in a future that could involve Cam. Guilt crushed hope.

"Mama won't call me in the mornings."

"They have phones in Mexico."

"Who's going to make me *sopes, tortillas, tamales?*"

His hand left hers and stroked her hip. "You always complained about the food making you more curvy than KESP allows."

"Who's going to take me to Christmas Mass at St. Agatha's?"

"I'll go with you."

"You? You hate church. You don't believe in God."

"But I love you," Cam said without pause. Her heart

sped up again. She gripped the napkin in her hand even harder. She couldn't remember the last time she'd heard him say that. She couldn't remember if she'd ever heard him say that. His thumb slowly stroked right below her rib cage. A tide of emotion overwhelmed her, a jumble of feelings. She couldn't separate one from another. Tears leaked again.

"I'll miss them."

He reached over and got a napkin from another table. "It's the right thing."

"There's nothing I can do, is there?"

Cameron's eyes met and held hers. He shook his head slowly.

If he could be so calm, perhaps there wasn't much to worry about. "Maybe she'll get a better job after they get settled. She's bilingual. She has a degree in psychology. Maybe she could get a Masters. I could help her research programs in Mexico City. I wonder—"

A single finger brushed her lips. "Shhh. Let her unpack."

"I wonder if you arresting Dolores could be the single best thing that ever happened to her."

Cam didn't move, but he got closer. His body heat, warmer. His breath stirred the hair near her ear. "Do you want to get a doggy bag?"

A shiver whispered up her spine. He hadn't forgotten either.

She was temped, very much so. Thoughts of work fought their way through yearning, and kept her on the straight and narrow. "The station calls."

Cameron looked at his own watch, and reality came

back into the focus. "Gotta go to the station myself." He waggled his eyebrows. "Got ninety minutes."

Yesenia had to laugh. Men were incorrigible. "I'll call you."

Something clicked into place. Something that had been out of sync for years. "I think I'd like that."

♥

FOR MORE THAN A WEEK, Cam and Jessie talked like old friends. Nothing more. He didn't push on her response to the words he'd worked long to push out, or on whether she was ready to give them a try, or what more he could do to win her over. Instead he listened to her seesaw back and forth between hope and despair.

Jessie asked for help with the house. Without hesitation, he rearranged his schedule and borrowed a pickup from Rivera in case he needed to move furniture. His wife was sitting on the steps of the Alsace house, sunglasses firmly in place. Her hair, pulled through a hole in her baseball cap, bounced when she turned toward him.

Even with decades-old cutoffs that predated their marriage and ratty Converse high tops, the pull was still there. He'd first fell for her because she was so resilient. So many girls he'd dated after high school had been clingy, afraid of everything; the L.A. gang problem, and losing him to gun violence, no matter how unlikely the possibility. Jessie took so much of that in stride. Probably because she'd grown up around those same gangs and guns. Because deportation was a much bigger worry than losing a boyfriend.

She'd needed him, even if she hadn't known it that first night in the station. Jessie had needed shelter from the storm of her family's demands and some honest-to-God fun. He'd been happy to provide both. Thrilled to bring a smile to her serious face. A little levity to a life of obligation.

He'd even admired that her ambition was much like his own. Determination to make something more of their humble beginnings. Until her drive to succeed came between them. Cameron banished the thought from his mind. They were beyond that and more mature than they'd been.

"Been inside?" he asked.

Her sigh was long, drawn out. "No. Let's go."

Jessie rose as slowly as an eighty year old woman with debilitating arthritis. Keys in hand, she twisted a rusty lock. The iron door opened with some protest. She fitted keys into a second lock, then a third, forcing the steel-reinforced door inward.

The inside of the house was a mirror of the day they'd helped Dolores and Reina move in. Used and discarded furniture littered the front rooms. The dining room table remained, but the chairs were gone. Kitchen cabinets stood half-empty. He pushed past his wife and inspected the bedrooms. The light pink carpet lay nearly bare. Faded patches and deep divots showed where furniture had stood, unmoved, for nearly a decade.

Like the home's previous owners, Jessie's mother and sister hadn't much cared about who was coming after them. With virtually no cleaning, they'd taken advantage of Jessie's unfailing reliability again. If he had any control, it would be the last time. There'd been so much hope when he and Jessie had bought this house. Hope that Dolores would figure out what she wanted in life. Hope that Reina would feel settled despite her status. Location didn't change people, he'd learned.

She joined him in the smaller of the two bedrooms. The one she'd shared with her sister between the separation and striking out on her own.

Turning to him, she said, "Should we keep it?"

"The house?"

"It's yours as much as mine."

"You want to rent it out? I figured you'd want to sell it." Forget the old. Start something new, he thought.

"So...I was thinking of moving in." She rushed on before he could say anything. "I'd buy you out, of course."

"What about your place?"

"It's been sold to someone else." There was a melancholy look around her eyes. He could see how much that apartment had meant to her. How much she'd wanted to strike out on her own in a place not drowning in memories. But when she'd used the money for her sister's lawyer, that dream had gone up in a wisp of smoke. "I wanted to buy a place this year. And since we already own this one and it has a sudden vacancy—"

"Do you want to live down here?"

"Here? In the *barrio*, you mean?"

Why did she deliberately misunderstand him? He'd always believed the best of her. Until he hadn't. "Near the freeway, I meant. Years ago you did that report on asthma clusters and heavy particulates."

"I'm sorry."

"Why do you always do that? Jump to the worst conclusion?"

She looked at the toes of her sneakers. Her foot rubbed the carpet one way, then another. "I don't know. Defense mechanism, maybe."

"I'm not the villain. I was probably stubborn, closed off—"

"Angry."

"I think I had a right to be. But it was because of what you did, not because of who you were."

She turned away, putting a period on discussion of the past. "I could get new windows. Maybe some kind of whole house filtration system."

Cam made a slow three sixty. Could he expand the dream of their future to include this house? It wasn't exactly a ranch in Toluca Lake.

"I'm single. It's about the size of my place. Plus, it has a yard," she continued.

"You could rent it while you think about it," he countered. "Give it a year. See if your sister and mom can stick it out."

Picking up a box of discarded clothes, she said, "Let's put the junk out for garbage pickup. I'll call the city for the big stuff."

"Should I call Ryan?"

Jessie shook her head, screwing up her face. Even under the glasses and hat, he could tell she wasn't itching for a reintroduction to his family. She'd always been uncomfortable with Ryan and his mom Bridget. Neither of them had been as welcoming as he would've liked.

She'd probably thought it was because she was

Mexican or from South L.A. It wasn't that. They were protective of Cam, thinking she didn't really love him. But she did, in her own way. All the other stuff had gotten in the way of that. He tabled Ryan, and pulled leather work gloves from his back pocket.

"What's first?" Most of Dolores' furniture couldn't be sold, saved, or even given away. It wasn't the fact that her family had left the discarded stuff that irritated him. He understood how quickly they'd needed to act once they'd decided on voluntary departure. It was that Jessie hadn't been left a note or a word of thanks for cleaning up her family's mess even if it was the last time.

For a couple of hours, they worked in tandem to pull apart the particleboard dresser, taking it from the house and stacking it on the tree lawn. Dori's old clothes joined the pile, tied up in dark black plastic. Boxes from the garage that had rotted through several winter rains went out as well.

With brisk efficiency of someone used to cleaning up others' messes, Jessie got a vacuum from her car. She sucked up all the dust and dirt left behind. He took a rag and cleanser from under the kitchen sink and wiped the cabinets, fridge, and counters.

When she wandered in, rolling the vacuum back toward the front door, he said, "Let that be. Let's see what's in here." He pulled open the refrigerator. Unlike the rest of the house, it was nearly empty. Cam lifted two Jarrito sodas from the shelf. Guava wasn't his favorite flavor, but he chugged it down, needing the water and sugar.

"Should I order delivery?" he asked after the growl of his stomach filled the quiet air.

Jessie laughed, shaking her head. "There's no delivery."

"What about pizza? That Indian place on Pico," he offered what was close by, offhand.

"There's no delivery to this neighborhood, Cameron," she said again.

"What are you talking about? I order in all the time."

"I'm sure restaurants are happy to serve North Hollywood now that it's full of hipsters and out priced families, right?"

She pulled another trash bag from the counter, and went out to the porch. Fine, he'd pick without her. Cameron pulled the phone from his pocket and called a pizza place in Larchmont, then the Indian place on Pico Boulevard. Frustrated, he called two different delivery services. By the end of the fourth call, he was pissed and hungry. Admittedly a bad combination.

Jessie came back in, pulling off gloves. "I put the dead plants in the green bin. The cracked flower pots are out too. Do you think I should—"

"They won't deliver."

"Mm, hm."

"How can you be so calm?"

"I told you this a half hour ago."

"One doesn't deliver south of Venice. The other won't go south of Pico."

"Why?"

"The second pizza manager hung up on me. Last time I eat there. I don't care what Rivera wants."

"The other excuses?"

"Not enough demand. Gang activity."

"There you have it, Cameron. How many times have I told you that life isn't fair, especially for the black and brown people down here?"

"This is Los Angeles. In the United States of America." Cameron realized he was shouting. He rolled back his indignation a little.

"I may not have been born here. But even I know there's no constitutional right to food delivery, Cameron."

"This is the second largest city in the country. Four million people live here."

"We have cars. We can go out."

"Have you covered this in KESP?"

"Not exactly. It's not the crime of the century, Cam. It's a little bit of economic injustice. It's cute that you're riled up on my behalf."

"Maybe if they put you behind a desk, you could cover real stories like this."

"Funny," she said, though her facial expression was exactly the opposite. "There are bigger issues, like the economic disparity of recent immigrants in Pacoima. Families have been exploited, living two or three to a thousand square foot bungalow. Lack of city services both there and here. Failing schools. Environmental pollution. Unsolved crimes. Police harassment. That's what I've covered. Whether Angelenos south of Pico or north of Sherman Way can get pizza in a half hour or less is not news."

"Maybe you're right," he said.

"I know you believe the world should be as fair and

honest as you, but it's not. In order to stay here, I've come to accept it. I had to."

He grabbed one of her hands in his, held it firm. "What does that mean for us? It's not you versus me, Jessie. I want us to be a team, like we used to be."

"Do you really think there can be a future for us, Cam?" she asked. Her voice was soft. She pulled off her glasses. Brown eyes, intense, sincere stared back at him.

Instead of answering her, he pulled her to him. "It's always been about us," he whispered into her hair. Then he kissed her. He'd tried restraint and that wasn't getting them anywhere. He needed to use everything he had. He wanted to drag her down to the living room floor, show her how good they could be together.

"I thought you were hungry," Jessie said, putting a millimeter of space between them.

"Found the perfect diet," he said. "I could feast on you all night."

Cameron watched her eyes go wide, the pupils expand until the brown was just a small ring. Something hit the floor. He glanced down for a moment. Work gloves. He pulled at her hands until he was sitting on a clean section of the carpet, her in his lap. Already hot as blazes, he pulled off his own t-shirt.

"What are we —"

"—Doing, Jessie? We're doing the one thing that's always worked for us." This time he kissed her hard. He pulled off the baseball cap, tossing it aside. Snaking his hands through her hair, he pulled the dark strands around them to block out the world that had always intruded on their relationship. She melted into him, and he took control.

He broke the kiss when the distraction of her nipples against his chest made it impossible to focus on her full lips and her tongue sweet with soda. "I want to see you," he said, pulling her bra and t-shirt over her head in a single movement. Jessie looked like she wanted to get lost in another kiss, but Cameron didn't want them to get swept away. He wanted them right here, grounded, knowing what this was between them.

Gently, he eased her from his lap, and laid her back against the soft pink pile. While he worked on the knots of her laces, he pulled together what he wanted to say to her. "You are," he began, easing off one sock and shoe, moving to the other, "the sexiest woman I've ever known."

"You don't have to—"

"But I do. It's true, Jessie." He tugged at the cutoffs, her underwear coming with them.

"The lights. Should we—"

"No, Jessie we shouldn't," Cameron said, sitting back on his haunches and admiring the woman before him. He fought with his need to devour her and her need to hear the words. Keeping his pants, socks, and shoes firmly on, he lay next to her. Propped on his elbow, he traced down the column of her throat with a single finger. "I love your skin."

Color rose on her cheekbones, where his finger had swept, on the tops of her breasts. "Even though…"

"There is no even though, Jessie. I love your body because it's so beautiful. Not in spite of anything." This talking was what she needed, but he broke off to give them a little bit of what else they needed. Using his free hand, he plumped her breast, then lowered his mouth. That small bit of flesh that was her nipple grew hard in his mouth. He curled his tongue around it. A moan escaped her. He looked to see his wife throw an arm across her eyes, arch her throat in arousal. "I love that I can make you as hard as you make me," he whispered, embarrassed by his own admissions. He'd asked her to give, but he was finding that it was harder than he thought.

She turned to him, her arms pulling at the back of his head for a kiss, seeking something like oblivion. To hell with the talking and the need for back and forth, he gave her what she needed.

An hour or two later, she turned to him. "What now?"

He wanted everything to end like a fairy tale. Have them ride off into the sunset. But this wasn't a movie. Sex was only the answer to a handful of questions. It hadn't been enough before, and wasn't enough now. He was too old to make that kind of mistake.

"Give me a month to convince you," he said.

ELEVEN

IF YESENIA HAD TO GUESS, she thought the last couple of weeks could have been called dating. Feeling Cam's eyes on her, she gave him the biggest smile she could muster, then turned to look back at the landscape passing by through the car window. He'd asked to take her out this afternoon.

Dating sounded juvenile to her ears, but there wasn't any other way to describe it. She hadn't told Cam this, but spending time with him, not so much talking, but kissing, and making out was a great distraction from worrying about her mother and sister. Not that they needed her to worry about them.

Mexico City wasn't the same place they'd left decades earlier. Their new neighborhood had high speed internet, a Wal-Mart, and a burgeoning middle class. Mama and Dori had Skyped with her every other day, finally putting the laptop she'd bought her sister to good use. And with the same big box stores they had in the states, her family had been able to furnish their apartment with stuff they hadn't been able to fit in the small rental van they'd driven from Los Angeles.

Through the computer screen, Mexico seemed so normal. What was abnormal, though, was being alone. Yesenia couldn't remember spending more than a night or two without a visit or a call in her entire life. Even with her own apartment, she was at Mama's house or Dori was at hers nearly one night out of three. When she wanted to pick up the phone, or drive over to Alsace, someone was always there. She regretted all the days she thought she'd be better off without her meddlesome, needy family.

Right now, she'd take a summons from her mama or a chance to bitch at Dori about Raul over navigating life without them. Cameron had slipped so easily into the chasm of loneliness, but it was still hard to believe that their fragile reunion would stick.

Her not-so-ex husband pulled over on a leafy residential street in Beverly Hills. She looked at the huge ficus trees shading the sidewalk, and the mansions on either side of the wide road.

"I thought we were going to lunch," she said. Cam had mentioned something about trying out food trucks that were popular around the city. There wasn't a boxy painted truck or cadre of folding chairs and tables in sight.

He came around to her side of the car and helped her out. "It's down there," he said, pointing toward Santa Monica Boulevard. Cam held her hand as they walked down Crescent Drive. She hoped her faded denim shorts and cotton espadrilles were appropriate. Not that a food truck was fancy, but she'd seen a lot of women in Beverly

Hills drink coffee in five hundred dollar designer outfits, their equally expensive bags at their feet.

A small sigh of relief escaped her when she got closer. She wasn't going to have to be *on*. Only food and a little conversation.

Food trucks had gotten inventive. When she was a kid, there were taco trucks. Now every continent was represented. And the word "fusion" was everywhere. There were food trucks galore and a sign announcing the city's semi-annual art show along Beverly Gardens Park.

"Cam?" she questioned her voice unsteady. Yesenia had nothing against art shows. It wasn't the kind of thing they'd done when they were dating that first time around. Back then it had been dinner, movie, make out session. Until he'd convinced her to move on to sex. They didn't need to replicate that non-adventurous pattern, though. That had ended in disaster. This time around, he was more interested in her and what made them work separate from the escape from overbearing mothers and the sex.

"I thought we'd look at some stuff after we eat," he said.

She lifted and dropped her shoulder in a shrug, and took in the hundreds of white tents. Yesenia hadn't been to the Beverly Hills Art Show since she'd covered a story about two Mexican artists featured here a few years ago.

He linked his fingers with hers. They looked at a few stalls with oil and watercolor paintings of California landscapes.

"You going to buy something?" she asked. Her mind flashed to the bare green walls of his studio apartment. He'd never been one for artwork. When they'd been together, she'd taken on the task of making their house a home. He was so different now than he'd been their first time around. Maybe he would put something up on the wall other than a TV. She'd like that, she realized. The idea that he could simply enjoy life more. Her heart thudded as she pictured a future, enjoying life with him.

Yesenia was yanked from her fantasy when Cam stopped short. "Take your pick," he said, pointing to the long line of brightly colored trucks. Everything from salad to a three course meal was for sale. The Maine lobster truck intrigued her. She hadn't traveled much in the U.S. When no one in the family had papers, her mama had been cautious about traveling. Avoiding spontaneous INS roadblocks had left them with few driving options. And they'd been too poor to fly.

Looking up, Yesenia took in the relentless sun. She'd always wanted to go to New England for the fall foliage, taste the kind of food they had on the other coast.

"Maine lobster," she said.

"That's my Jessie." Cam put his arm across her shoulders and led her over to the truck. After he purchased her food, he started laughing. Weaving their way toward a free table, Cam couldn't stop. If she hadn't thought he was possibly laughing at her, it would have been contagious.

"I don't get what's so funny," she said, her tone a little sharper than she'd have liked. The combination of laughter and food sometimes made her flash back to those times her mom hadn't packed the right kind of lunches for her and Dolores. Embarrassment had stained her cheeks each time she'd had to pull out homemade tortillas to scoop up the meat and beans her mother had prepared.

When he could control himself, he answered. "You got lobster tacos."

"I really wanted to try the Maine lobster," she said defensively. The muscles of her face tightened as her eyebrows came together like they did when she was a kid and couldn't translate some local idiom fast enough. "It's supposed to be way different than the Pacific spiny lobster," she tried to explain.

"You think tacos are traditional."

Heat spread through first her chest, then crept up her neck. Yesenia's face would be next. "They're not?"

"Wouldn't think so. Lobster boils. Lobster rolls. Lobster salad, yes."

She turned away, hiding her shame from Cam. She'd gone to college. Gotten a job. She was trying her damnedest to live the American dream. But before she'd met Cam, she probably hadn't been more than fifty miles from Los Angeles as a kid. Except for that hellish Texas border crossing, she hadn't been out of California since she'd arrived. That hadn't changed after citizenship or their separation. Not with a job hyper-focused on local stories happening within driving distance from the studio.

When she turned back from her people-watching pretense, Cam had devoured his *traditional* lobster roll.

He touched her hand. "You got quiet there."

Five years ago, she would have shook this off, pretended it didn't matter. But she wanted him to know who she *really* was, not the expertly wrapped package she wanted the world to see.

"It's stupid," she equivocated. "I don't feel like I belong here a lot of times. It's not your fault, you were kidding, but it hit me right here," she tapped between her breasts, "when you made fun of the tacos."

"Baby." Cam's voice was a low, hoarse rumble. "I didn't mean it that way at all. I love that about you, the many ways you're different from me. I didn't mean to hurt you. I'd never do that on purpose."

"No big deal," she said. Though his words, his apology were a big deal. Changing the subject, she asked, "Are you eyeing my tacos?"

"You gonna eat all three?"

Shame forgotten for a moment, she had to smile. No matter what happened, this man never lost his appetite. She rolled her eyes, gave him one, and ate the other two before he got any ideas. For non-traditional tacos, they weren't so bad.

"You ready?" Cam asked after he'd bussed the table.

"Sure."

"I want to stop by booth…" He pulled a small notepad from his front pocket. "Two forty-six."

"Who's there?" she asked. Cam had few friends when they'd been married. None had been artists. She tried to envision him with nosering-wearing, tattoo-bearing people. Nope, couldn't do it. Maybe he'd met some up on the NoHo arts district where his apartment was. With the new, improved Cam, anything was possible.

"Sophie Reid," he said, tugging her along. Well, the improbable artist had a name, was a woman. Her heart beat a little faster.

Skipping all the booths in between the food and their destination, they came upon a woman in purple overalls.

Cam cleared his throat to get the artist's attention, and she turned.

Yesenia's skin prickled with jealousy. Artist Sophie was cute. Even the purple tipped strawberry blonde hair suited her. Light eyes sparkled under her bangs.

"Ryan must have told you, right?" The woman shook her head, waves bouncing around her face. "He couldn't keep one little secret. I wanted to try out a show without a big audience." She sported a petulant pout. Yesenia's heart slowed with dread. This was exactly the kind of woman Ryan would probably try to set up with Cam. Someone who would complement him better, laid back, down to earth to his tight shouldered, wound up nature. Ryan had always said she and Cam were too alike.

"Hey, bro," Cam said. His brother appeared as if out of nowhere, two sweating water bottles in hand. He kissed Sophie full on the mouth. Yesenia's heart gave a squeeze, then released. Jealousy that had fizzed in her veins moments ago spilled like soda from an overturned can.

"I'm Yesenia Morales," she said, holding out her hand toward Ryan's woman when it didn't look like she was going to get an introduction from either of the guys. They pretended to act flustered for a second, but looked relieved that they didn't have to tackle who she was or why she was with Cam.

"Yesenia?" She could see Sophie rooting around her memory like she was supposed to know who Yesenia was.

"I'm Cameron's ex. If you've met Bridget, I'm sure she's mentioned me," she said, then immediately wanted to stuff the stupid words back into her mouth. If she was so important in Cam's life, why hadn't he mentioned they were dating? The entire situation was starting to make her uncomfortable. After years of trying to fit in at school, at work, in this country, she hated feeling out of step with everyone else.

"Jessie?"

Yesenia nodded. No one in the Becker family called her by her given name. "Right," Sophie said brightly, her voice and manners impeccable. The raising of her pierced eyebrow was the only indication that she'd been given less than favorable information. Not letting on as to the unflattering picture Bridget had probably painted of "Jessie" as a needy woman unable to let go. Ryan had traded up with this one. No poor immigrant girl for that up and comer. Bridget must be over the moon. "Nice to meet you." Sophie's handshake was firm.

"You paint?" Yesenia asked the obvious, ready to change the subject. She studied the bright colored acrylics and oils hanging in the booth. Another two paintings graced easels. Of course Sophie had time for art. People with money always did.

"Sort of a hobby, I guess," Sophie answered. "I'm really a make-up artist by trade."

Yesenia studied Sophie's face. She did a great job with the nude look. She wished this girlfriend of Ryan's would come to KESP and give pointers. She was over the porcelain doll look the station bosses insisted viewers wanted. Mentally, she changed the subject. Years ago, she'd realized there was nothing to be gained from comparing herself to *gringos*. It was like looking at fashion magazines. She'd never be a white, native-born American woman. There was no use making comparisons.

Her hard won resolve was gone in an instant when a stunning blonde joined the group, a small girl who looked about four or five by her side. She kissed Sophie on the cheek. "You asked. I produced. Daddy's golfing."

Sophie bent to kiss the little girl and listen to the child's enthusiastic chatter.

Turning to Yesenia, the woman held out her perfectly manicured hand. "Selena," she said. It was obvious that Selena and Sophie were sisters. Selena's smooth voice and manners were nearly identical, but she looked more like the money they'd probably come from. Yesenia squashed the inner reporter's urge to ask questions. She'd do the right thing and probe Cam later. But still she was dying to know how someone like Sophie had ended up with Ryan. Where the Reid sisters were from. How Sophie had ended up with a union job and didn't become a lady who lunched.

Instead of launching into a litany of questions, hearing her own thick accent compared to their even California tones, she introduced herself again, leaving the separation out, this time. She didn't want to brave any more raised eyebrows today. The little girl tugged at her mother's white chiffon dress, shooting meaningful looks up at her mother and pointing purposefully.

Sophie squatted again. "What's up, Maddie?"

"Momma promised me I could look at the cactus."

"I'm talking to Auntie Sophie, right now," Selena said. "In ten minutes, we can go."

Sophie stood and the sisters whispered something then laughed.

"I'll do it," Yesenia said, surprising herself. She wasn't

normally the first to volunteer to entertain children. But her discomfort with one small child would be easier than being with a bunch of well-off folks with their art and "inside" jokes.

Selena turned to her. "There's no need, I'm trying to__"

"Jessie, you don't — " Cam interjected.

"Oh, it's okay," Yesenia said, pushing away from the white canvas tent. They all looked at each other, but no one said anything as Maddie introduced herself.

"Jessie," she said to the girl, and then held out her hand.

As trusting as only a child could be, Maddie grasped Yesenia's fingers and led her away. Following the little girl in her pink sequin shoes, Yesenia sighed in relief. Uncomfortable with Cam's family, she'd do anything to avoid one lovey-dovey couple and possibly embarrassing questions she had no desire to answer.

The little girl's chatter washed over her, but its soothing hum wasn't enough to take away her unease. It had taken years for her to go from being a nervous wreck to relative calm around Cam's family. Bridget had grudgingly accepted their marriage. Ryan had been too busy, first with his old fianceé Jocelyn, then with climbing the corporate ladder to give her and Cam too much grief.

Toward the end, holiday dinners were...if not pleasant...then bearable. Everyone acted predictably, and she kept quiet. But two new faces—and rich ones at that—was more than she could take, along with the worry about her own family and her tenuous relationship with Cam at the forefront of her thoughts.

Maddie tugged at her hand as they got closer to the manicured desert gardens.

"Cactus!" The girl reached out her hand toward a sprig of red erupting from a plant.

"I see the plants." Yesenia squatted like Sophie had, grabbing hold of the girl's arm. "You have to be careful. These plants can sting you."

"What?"

Yesenia cursed her accent. "They can poke, hurt you."

"I want to walk through them," Maddie said, shaking off her loose hold. "I'll be careful, I promise."

Yesenia let her go. How much damage could a small girl do?

❤

"WHICH ONE IS YOUR MOTHER?" A woman Cam's mother's age clutched at onyx beads around her neck with one hand and practically dragged an unhappy Maddie along in the other.

He looked at Sophie's sister's little girl. Her face was tear-streaked. Where was Jessie? His head whipped around. Had his wife been injured? Worse? There she was, lingering a couple of steps behind the indignant woman, shaking in her straw and cotton sandals.

Maddie pointed toward Selena. Seeing her upset daughter, Sophie's sister was out of her chair in an instant. "Honey, what's wrong?"

"I fell—"

The bead clutching woman cut the child off. "I'm sorry to say your nanny is doing a terrible job." The woman pointed an accusatory finger at Jessie. "She let this girl jump into a cactus patch. The child could have lost an eye, permanently scarred her face."

Selena leaned down toward the child. "Honey," she murmured and smoothed the damp hair from the girl's face. "Tell Momma what happened."

"I didn't hurt myself."

Selena raised an eyebrow.

"I jumped off the bench."

"What did I say about jumping from high places?"

Maddie's lip poked out in mutinous preschooler defiance. "You said benches were for sitting, not for jumping. It was dangerous. But *I* was careful," she said, her pronunciation of the words a clear imitation of her mother's warning.

Cameron moved between the family and the woman. "It's all under control," he said, dismissing her. "Thanks."

"But isn't she going to be reprimanded?" He looked down at a woman whose opinion was probably rarely questioned. He was supremely glad he wasn't in the midst of an investigation. Witnesses like this always thought they knew best, though they'd never done a lick of police work. Most officers deferred, taking the easy path. He'd never done that.

"Why?" he asked point blank.

"Because—"

Cam didn't let her finish. There was no point. "The child defied her mother, and she'll be dealt with," he said with finality, ready to turn his back.

"What about her?" The woman pointed toward Jessie.

"What *about* her?" Cameron pushed up his sunglasses,

and crossed his arms. It worked like it always had. He'd learned long ago at the academy that the appearance of authority was nearly as important as having a gun.

"She–"

He held out his hand. Jessie linked her hand with his. Good girl. "She's my wife."

The woman's lips pursed into a maroon lipstick O.

Everyone in Sophie's booth and the surrounding areas had quieted, watching the confrontation unfold. "But–" The woman's voice was a loud, protesting shriek in the near silence.

"There are no buts, here. Just my wife and family. I'd ask that you leave us, not spoil our day more than you already have."

There were nods of assent from others at the park who went back to looking at art. Defeated, the woman opened and closed her mouth a few times, a strong imitation of the koi in the nearby pond. Cam continued to give her the hard stare. Dissatisfied, she finally stalked off.

"Sorry about that," Selena said into the awkward silence. "Maddie is a little daredevil in pink shoes." She smoothed the hair of the girl in her lap. Maddie looked as docile as a kitten at the moment. "One minute she's like this. The next minute, I'm calling nine-one-one."

Sophie spoke next. "I'm not sure what to say. I hope she didn't hurt your feelings. I hate it when things like that happen. Just when I think L.A. is so liberal, I get slapped in the–"

"It's okay," Jessie said. Her voice was calm, but the wrinkle between her eyebrows, and the tight lips said anything but to Cam.

Ryan came back, this time with coffee. Observing what must have looked like an awkward silence, he spoke. "What did I miss?"

"Nothing, bro. We gotta shove off," Cam said.

"Good luck with your show," Jessie said to Sophie. "I hope you sell a lot."

"Thanks. I'm so sorry. I wish–"

Jessie shook her head, cutting the woman off. Then Ryan, Selena and Sophie turned to a well-heeled group that came to admire the paintings.

Their walk from the fair to the car was silent. Jessie leaned against the car, making no attempt to get in. "You stood up for me."

Those five words hurt like a punch in the gut. He wanted to say that he'd stood up for her before, be he hadn't always. He'd let her fend for herself with Reina, and Dolores; when Bridget had pointed her accusatory finger, and when Ryan had shaken his head.

"I've let you down too many times."

His ego wanted her fervent denial. But he got the honesty he deserved in the chin that lowered to her chest.

He stopped fiddling with the keys in his pocket, and came face to face with his wife. *"Lo siento,"* he pushed through his lips. The foreign words tasted right on his tongue. The awkwardness he sometimes felt in Spanish wasn't there because he was saying what he needed to say.

"It wasn't your fault, that woman–"

"That's not what I'm sorry for," he said. The words he needed to say stuck in his throat for a long moment. He swallowed. "I'll never let you down again. I will always be by your side, on your team, in your corner. Whatever you need."

He watched her face transform from worry and embarrassment to something he wanted to think was admiration, if not love.

TWELVE

MAYBE IT WOULD HAVE BEEN best to let Jessie have time to take in all the changes in her life. But he couldn't stay away. Now that his wife was back in his life, he wanted to make the change permanent. Extracting a blue sweater from his small closet, he pulled it over his undershirt.

Ryan had said he should wear blue, so he'd gotten a bunch of blue things and stashed them in his closet. Something about bringing out his eyes. Plugging his ears and singing "la, la, la" had made it difficult to hear everything his brother had said. But he thought dressing better out of respect for Jessie was the gist of it.

"Come to brunch," Cam said as soon as Jessie opened the door to her apartment. Her squint said she was surprised to see him. The small slight pricked him like a doctor's booster shot. But he shrugged it off. Jessie's state of undress helped him a whole lot with forgetting the pain.

If her routine was anything like it had been when they'd been together, the short robe meant she'd just come out of the shower. He stepped closer than propriety allowed into a common vestibule. Took a deep breath. Yep, he'd guessed right. She smelled like the lemon verbena cream he'd helped her smooth on a time or ten. Damned lotion brought back a bunch of memories of what had happed after her showers. And the two of them needing another when they were done. He took another step forward. They needed to move this party back through her door into the apartment.

"Let's skip brunch," he said, pushing the door closed with the sole of his shoe. Starting at the back of her neck, he smoothed his way down the satin lapels.

"Was it only us?"

That halted his movements. "I invited my mom. I mentioned it when I dropped you off."

"Bridget will eat me alive if we're late," she said, brushing his hands away and pulling the robe a little tighter. Sighing, he stepped back.

"Let's go then." He'd come here to take her out, keep her busy. Without her mom cooking and her sister sulking in that now empty house, he knew she'd be at loose ends. Cam broke eye contact and his mind went from honorable to not in the second it took to take her in again. As he'd silently hoped, he could see her nipple poking against the silky smooth fabric. Suddenly he didn't give a damn about food or family, his or hers.

"Can I eat you instead?" Cam said. His thoughts about why he was here and where they needed to go got muddled as the blood rushed from his brain, downward. She turned on her heel and strode to her kitchen sink. He watched her as she lazily turned on the tap, running the sponge under the water. Seconds later, she was wiping at the already spotless counter when he put his hands on her. This was one of those times he wished he were better with words. He wanted to tell her that he loved the feel of the silky fabric over her shoulders. That she shivered with want for him while she feigned reserve.

Cam knew a mixed message when he saw one. He pressed his advantage. In a second, he put his lips on her neck, slipped a hand under robe cupping the cheek of her sweet little ass. Something between a sigh and moan escaped her and she pushed him away. Jessie wrapped her arms around her body protectively, squeezing her thighs closed.

To him it looked like she was turned on. But the clued in part of his brain could see the signs of her internal battle. Her inner censor was winning. "Cameron Owen Becker. Would you talk to your mother with that mouth?"

"No. But I want to lick you with it, suck you with it."

"Cam—"

"I'm giving you a choice," he said, holding her face, meeting her eyes with his. Hoping against hope she'd pick him over his mother.

She looked wary. "Between what and what?"

"I already told you," he said. Ah, damn. She turned his insides to mush. All that tawny skin. Those straight black brows above her expressive brown eyes. Her lids closed, sweeping eyelashes over high cheekbones. He didn't want her to make a choice.

When her full lips pursed as if to speak, he plucked the sponge from her, tossing it blindly. He pushed her up against the counter and kissed her, hard. Boldly, Cam inserted his leg between her thighs. It took everything he had to keep his hands above her waist. Then she squeezed her thighs in a vice grip around his leg. With that squeeze, all bets were off.

He'd been ready for food until she opened for him. Leaning in, he stroked her tongue with his. Used to taking command, he nearly came when she nipped his lower lip, then soothed it with her tongue. Her hands gripped at his butt, then moved—first toying with his belt, then cupping his erection through the fabric of his pants. She found the tip, and pushed her thumb against the ridge.

He pulled back, leaving a half inch between them. "Jesus, Jessie. What in the hell are you doing?"

"What you asked." His mind went blank. What in the hell had he asked? To taste her? To make love to her with his mouth. "For me to be more aggressive."

Shit. That. She'd gone from school girl to siren in the blink of an eye. And damned if it wasn't the hottest thing he'd ever experienced.

Cam didn't know what he'd expected when he'd pushed her up against the counter, but this wasn't it.

"What's wrong?" Jessie said. How long had he been standing there?

"Nothing."

Jessie pulled at the tie to her robe, but Cam grabbed the ties she would have spread open. He'd need more than ten minutes to delve into this side of Jessie. He liked the give and take. He was figuring out how he was going to reach his Luddite of a mother who didn't have a cell, when there was a hitch in her breath.

"We can't do this," she said in direct contradiction to the breath that panted the words against his ear.

"Why?" He really wanted to know. Because he'd already undressed her in his mind. Images of hard brown nipples straining toward him, breasts bouncing, the curve of her hips and belly as they ground against his body, came together in one gorgeous montage in his head. His only hang up was logistics.

"It's not right that we do this, keep doing this if we don't have a future together."

"You could fix that," he proposed, sliding a hand under the robe, catching a nipple with his thumb. Unless she did something to stop this, he wouldn't–couldn't. To hell with being on time. The feel of her flesh, hard against soft, made the blood leave his brain in a whoosh. A zipper rubbing against his flesh let him know exactly where the blood had gone.

Jessie did what he couldn't. She pulled away. "Let's go eat with your mother."

Oh, hell. Brunch it was.

Ten minutes later, Jessie came down the stairs dressed like a good Catholic school girl in her Sunday best. The blue, white, and yellow striped dress covered her from collar bone to knees. Every one of her dark brown hairs was smoothed back into a conservative ponytail. Despite the wrapping, he still wanted to abandon brunch for what was underneath.

Damned separation. Why had he ever agreed to it? Some time for them both to lick their wounds. He'd never thought it would last more than a few months. As those months stretched into years, it got harder and harder to think of a way to bridge the gap that had grown between them. Their careers, their families seemed like two of the worst reasons to have abandoned their marriage. But hindsight was twenty-twenty.

Grabbing her hand, he pulled her from the apartment before he ended up using all the tools in his arsenal to change her mind. Breath calm, thoughts in check, Cam drove over to the restaurant on Third Street.

Jessie laughed. A deep and genuine belly laugh filled the car when she glanced through the window at the one word restaurant name, Toast. "Bridget hasn't changed?"

His mother was infamous for eating dry, inexpensive toast during regular Sunday brunches with her sons. Didn't want to put them out or strain their wallets, she claimed. "I thought this restaurant would suit," he said.

Thanks to Jessie's restraint, they were early enough to avoid the long line of hipsters that usually clogged the sidewalk outside the café. Once at their table, he watched Jessie down her third mug of coffee in as many minutes. She was about to flag the busboy for a refill, when he grabbed her hand.

"What's wrong?"

"I'm thirsty," she said. His wife didn't look parched, but irritable from all the caffeine rushing to her head.

"It'll be fine," he said. Rebuilding the mess they'd made of their marriage was a painstaking process. It started with winning back her trust in the bedroom and out. Then, showing he would bend over backwards to make it work this time. His family was the next hurdle. Ryan was a piece of cake compared to his mother. He wanted to set the tone that reconnecting his ex with his mother was a bridge to cross, not a hurdle to jump, or a mountain to climb.

"Gee, really. Last time I checked, your mother hated me."

"That's not true," he said.

"I'm not your biggest fan, dear," Bridget said before she plopped into a chair. He'd been so focused on Jessie that he hadn't seen his mother or that comment coming. Cam flagged down the waiter, for himself this time. After that, *he* was going to need something to get through this.

❤

DESPITE THAT RED-EYE, a shot of espresso in regular coffee, Yesenia felt incredibly tired, downright bone weary, in fact. For short glimpses of time in the last weeks, especially after his confrontation with that woman in Beverly Hills, she could see a future with Cameron in a starring role. But sitting here next to Bridget, his sharp-tongued mother, reconciliation seemed far, far away.

"You planning to take my son for another walk down the aisle?" Bridget asked, while Cameron ordered a double espresso.

Sitting back, Yesenia crossed one leg over the other, deliberately taking her time with the answer. She wasn't the shrinking violet she'd been all those years ago. She met her mother-in-law's snark with sarcasm. "I don't see why it would be a good idea," she retorted. "Since we met up again, I got stuck on an elevator, my sister got arrested, and my family moved back to Mexico." She remembered that Mrs. Becker had been a sports nut. "I'm not batting a thousand. Maybe I'd be better without Cam in my life."

Yesenia didn't dare look at Cam. She kept her eyes squarely trained on his mother. Bridget's mouth was the very definition of backtracking. "He does need to settle down," Bridget said. "I'd like to see both my boys happy."

Was that a hedge? Yesenia decided to prod her a little. She already had Bridget as a mother-in-law. There was nothing to lose. "What kind of woman do you think would be perfect for him?" she asked because it obviously wasn't her.

Bridget looked from Yesenia to Cameron and back again. It was going to be a boxing match. She wished Cam had warned her this morning. She would have made sure to wear protective gear, bring her gloves. Damn. She'd just have to bare knuckle it.

"Someone young enough to give me two or three grandkids," Bridget finally answered.

One punch in the gut for being old. She'd always wanted Cam's children, but never saw how she could stop working to care for a new family when she'd always had the old one to support. But Yesenia wasn't on the ropes yet, she pushed a little harder. "And?"

"Someone who can stay home and nurture those kids. I couldn't do it after my husband died. But I worked for families that could. It made for better kids."

Bridget's one-two punch was precise. His mom had jabbed at Yesenia's ambition all the while painting herself as a martyr with her woe-as-me story of having to clean houses when her own boys were kids. Muhammad Ali had nothing on this woman.

Though without tact, nothing Cam's mother had said had been untrue. In a weird way, she kind of missed Bridget. Rarely did she encounter a "tell it like it is" woman who wasn't afraid of what anyone thought of her.

Yesenia had to admire a woman who faced down the tragedy of losing a husband, and raised two wonderful men. She'd never taken an eye off her boys, and they'd both grown up to be loving, responsible men. One of whom had been her lover and protector until she'd pushed him away.

Ignoring years of manners, she put her elbows on the table, sunk her head into her hands. Might as well get comfortable if she was going to be in for all twelve rounds.

Unprompted, Bridget continued. "Someone who loves my son for who he is. Even if he does have a stick up his law-abiding ass, I know deep down there—" Bridget jabbed Cam's chest. "—he feels deeply. I want a daughter-in-law who didn't break his heart." The knockout punch. Bridget had delivered it like a champ. Broken? But he'd wanted to break up as much as she did, right? He'd said she betrayed him. What she'd done was nearly unforgivable. That he wanted a divorce. Was her memory faulty? Had he really frozen her out or was his behavior a response to the way she'd treated him? Damned if she knew anything at this point. She was punch drunk.

Yesenia looked at her husband. For one heart-stopping second, his guard was down and she saw what she hadn't seen for all those years. With a crashing realization that stole her breath, it hit her. She'd done something she'd never intended, never meant to do. She'd broken his heart.

THIRTEEN

ALL THE FIGHT LEFT HER. At once, Yesenia's straw-berry banana Belgian waffle was as tasteless as Bridget's dry toast. She didn't want to spar with his mom anymore. She needed time to think. Had their separation been one big misunderstanding? It couldn't be possible. He'd walked away, dry-eyed. Rebuilt his career from where she'd left it, broken. He'd probably even dated. No man as attractive as Cam could have been alone all that time.

She'd been the one devastated by his anger and mistrust. His lack of understanding about her family. Wanting to push away from the table, to go home and tend to her own wounds, it was nearly impossible to stay put, waiting for the check. She needed time to figure out if she could help Cam heal from the damage Bridget said she'd inflicted. Figure out if it was her job to help him. Figure out if he even wanted her help.

Turning her head slightly, she tried to furtively sneak glances at the man she'd fallen in love with, married, and left. Cam looked fine. He was tucking into a breakfast burrito with such relish, you'd never know the woman right next to him had laid him out emotionally.

As soon as she could, without appearing rude, Yesenia stood.

"Cam, I need to get home."

"I hope I didn't scare you off," Bridget said. Yesenia's antannae weren't finely tuned enough to figure out if his mom was sincere. In an instant, she decided it didn't matter.

"No, I need to check in at work," she said.

"Figures." Bridget put her balled up napkin on the table, then pulled an outdated phone from her purse. She squinted at the tiny keys, pressing them slowly and deliberately. Yesenia excused herself to the ladies' room. Fortunately, by the time she came back to the table, Ryan and his girlfriend appeared to pick up Bridget. For once, she wasn't even annoyed at her mother-in-law's intermittent refusal to drive in Los Angeles. Her own mother's undocumented status and lack of driver's license had made her a sometimes unwilling chauffer. But Bridget's reliance on her sons had always been a power play, through and through.

If she hadn't seen his guard slip for that single moment, Yesenia wouldn't have believed Bridget. But Cam didn't even look at her when he pulled to her door.

"Gotta get to work, myself," he said uncharacteristically drumming his fingers on the steering wheel.

"I don't really have to work. I only wanted to leave before things got too heavy."

"Not today." Cam only looked her way for a second, depositing a dry kiss on her cheek. He didn't meet her eyes. Well, her timing had been off then. Bridget had killed that morning's mood—dead.

"Are you sure?"

Yesenia was disappointed. She'd gotten used to being pursued. Pushing him out the door after a hot and heavy make out session. What would she do if he walked away?

"See you." He was flicking at his phone before she even stepped into the vestibule. No watchful eyes making sure she was safe.

Like a boxer who'd taken an uppercut, there was only the thinnest scab protecting their reconciliation. She *and* Cam had made a disaster of their marriage. They'd been immature and ill-equipped to deal with marriage's inevitable clashes. Maybe Cam's inadvertent leak of details from a confidential investigation, and her subsequent airing of a story that killed the cock-fighting sting dead was a bigger debacle than most couples faced, but with their family's urging, they'd turned away from each other.

She could see now that their troubles could have brought them closer together, made their marriage stronger. But they'd let the naysayers sever the frail ties they'd woven. Unless one of them did something, their reconciliation would be derailed like their marriage had been. And something told her, this would be their last chance.

Retreating to her comfy couch, Yesenia wallowed for a good long time, her wall clock ticking away the seconds, before the muffled sound of a phone ringing came from her purse.

"Cam?" she spoke hopefully into the receiver. Hoping

he'd do what he'd always done, make the first move to bridge the gap between them.

"Ernesto Barrero here," the voice said. Work.

Pushing the personal from her mind, she spoke. *"Lo siento. ¿Que pasó?"*

"You still friendly with your ex?"

Though Ernesto couldn't see her, Yesenia stood wary of what was coming next, but wanting to use her height to its maximum advantage even if it only made her feel more in control. "What happened?" she asked again.

"LAPD is letting Mitch Rasmussen turn himself in on the sly. They'll process him quick on a Sunday then let him go. No perp walk. No cameras. It'll be like it never happened."

"Wow."

"And the LAPD is letting a third councilman go."

Yesenia sat back down and racked her brain. She'd been so busy focusing on Dolores' mess that she'd heard only as much about the Rasmussen story as her viewers. Reading Ernesto's copy had been all she'd done. *City council members arrested in vice prostitution ring,* had been the opening line. The new, young reporter had done all the legwork on the story. "I thought they'd been charged."

"The two that were arrested, yes. They may even resign." She could hear Ernesto shuffling through some papers. "But there was a third arrest on Thursday night. Chas Hastings from the third district."

"But his dad was the district attorney and—"

"Exactamente. We think he put in a few well-placed calls. And bingo! He's gonna get out of jail this afternoon.

They're gonna give Hastings and Rasmussen the special treatment today."

Yesenia's heart raced. Involuntarily she sat forward, pressing her face more firmly into the phone. This was career gold. "A city corruption scandal will catch on like wildfire over this. I smell recall," she said. If it happened once, it happened a thousand times: an entitled public official took the easy way out. And next thing they knew, they were bounced from office. Her name in front of a story like that. She could hear the VO/SOT, read the headlines: Yesenia Morales of KESP broke the story of LAPD's special treatment program.

Ernesto spoke again, breaking into her thoughts. "Here's where you come in." The papers rattled again. She wondered if it was for effect. Her boss had a mind like a steel trap. He had to, given that the nature of his job as news director was to write and rewrite news instantly, judge which stories would stay or go. She had seen him rewrite entire newscasts without referring to any notes. "Lieutenant Cameron Becker is on deck to make the arrests and push the guys out the back door."

Mystery solved. Ernesto hadn't called her because of her skills, or for the career-making impact. He'd called her because of her ex. Plausible deniability had probably gone out with window when she'd answered the phone, breathing Cam's name.

"He's my ex," she said slowly, cautiously, emphasizing the last syllable.

"Didn't look so 'ex' by the elevators," Ernesto said.

"We...I..." Her private life was private. But that

earlier slip of the tongue had thrown a fork, stick–dammed English idioms–whatever, into things.

"I heard you answer the phone with his name."

So much for hoping he'd missed that.

"Look," Ernesto continued. "I heard the story about the exclusive you got all those years ago. How you exposed that undercover investigation into the celebrity-backed cock fighting and betting ring. Jumped you from reporter to weekend anchor."

"So–"

Here it comes.

"I'd love for you to become a permanent addition to the nightly news."

Which had been off the table since she'd been reading copy and not reporting on the story. She'd bowed out, citing personal issues. And they'd never made the connection with Dolores, thank goodness. But her readiness for the desk had been questioned from day one. Her chance to fix the past weeks was on the table. Game. Set. Match.

She ended the call with a noncommittal grunt. She punched in Cameron's cell. One ring turned to four. There was no response. He must be in the thick of things. She needed to talk to him. To explain what she was about to do.

Putting the phone back in her purse, she ran to the bathroom and put her full face on. Slipping out of mom-pleasing flats and into professional heels, she ran out the door. Like she'd done hundreds of times before, she pointed her Jeep in the direction of Hollywood division. On the way, Ernesto assured her by phone that a cameraman and intern would meet her there, satellite truck ready for immediate broadcast.

At every stop light she dialed, but got no answer from Cam.

She pulled up behind the KESP truck on Homewood Avenue, a block away and not visible from LAPD's Hollywood division. If they were going to ambush someone, they never situated the satellite truck near an entrance or exit. In L.A. everyone was looking for a camera. There was still something to be said for the element of surprise. People often told the truth first, and lied later. But if the truth were captured on film, it was hard to make up that lie….

When she approached, the cameraman Lyndon Turney had the transmitter extended. The intern, one of dozens she'd met during her tenure, was loading the camera with a fresh battery and assembling the waist pack.

"What do we need?" Lyndon asked. He liked to know what b-roll was needed, and what shots were priority. They'd do her stand up last.

"Chas Hastings and Mitch Rasmussen have 'get out of jail free' cards." Nothing more needed to be said. If they'd done this kind of story once, they'd done it a thousand times. Their job was to turn a quiet exit into a perp walk. Get the politicians on film leaving jail. Leave the image of police, arrest, and wrongdoing in the minds of viewers.

Lyndon looped the belt and hoisted the camera. They started the walk east toward Wilcox when her phone vibrated.

Cameron.

For two rings, she considered ignoring it. He couldn't be angry with her this time. He hadn't been the one to tip her off. Ernesto had gotten this one fair and square.

"Yesenia Morales," she answered.

"Sorry about Bridget," he said. She lifted a finger toward Lyndon and the intern, halting their procession. She walked a few feet away, seeking and finding a bit of privacy next to an overgrown bougainvillea.

"I'm on Homewood," she said.

She could hear Cameron's intake of breath. Then a long pause followed. "Why?"

"Hastings and Rasmussen are getting out in five minutes."

"Don't do this, Jessie." Cameron's voice was steel.

"You didn't tip me off. Ernesto did."

"Who's gonna believe that?" he asked. "It's only me and Rivera on this one."

"Then your partner's a snitch."

"No way it was her."

"If it wasn't one of you, then there's a leak in your shop. This is legitimate news. Someone inside doesn't want these two getting the special treatment. If I weren't talking to you, I'd think you were the leak."

"Seriously. You think I'd jeopardize my position, now?"

"You hate the idea that some perps get treated better than others."

Cam chose silence over denial.

"I can let our citizens know that. Maybe they can agitate for a police chief who doesn't do favors, vote for city council members who don't flout the law." There was more silence than static on the line. "Cam?"

"It's up to you, Jessie," Cameron said with finality. A double beep let her know he'd ended the call.

"Boss man?" Lyndon asked.

"My LAPD contact," she said. She closed her eyes for a prolonged moment. If she did as Cam asked, she was going to have to put a story together. Something plausible.

It was like bad karma. Here she was, all these years later having to make the same decision all over again. The only difference is that she had the foresight to know what lay behind door number one and door number two. It was like standing on stage during *Sabado Gigante*.

"What's the deal?" The intern was asking this time.

Career or love. It was that simple. And that complicated.

"The release has been delayed an hour," she lied, crossing her fingers behind her back. As if that one gesture would save her career. It was only a matter of time before the truth came out. She could only kick that can down the road for a small while.

"Oh, man," the intern responded. The starch had gone out of him. He traipsed back to the van, deflated.

"Gonna finish World Eleven," Lyndon said, taking the camera from his shoulder and pivoting one hundred eighty degrees.

For a long moment, Yesenia was confused.

"Angry Birds."

Right. Lyndon played one game or another every moment there was downtime. Maybe she should take up video games. She was about to have a lot of free time.

She'd tipped her hand. The truth was she'd lost her shark instinct after what she'd done to Cam. Yes, she'd take the promotion and the money. But she'd lost the scent for blood in the water. She'd done a great job pretending. Chasing the same stories as everyone else, but this was a field for hunters. If she lost site of the prey, her career would die of starvation. News was a hungry beast that needed to be fed twenty-four hours a day. The hand that had held the microphone under her arm dropped, dangling loosely at her side.

An hour from now, she'd have to go through the motions. Pretend they'd been fooled. Go back to Ernesto. She was toast.

FOURTEEN

"TALK TO ME," Jessie said Sunday night at Cam's studio. It was near midnight by the time he had gotten home. She'd been sitting in the lobby, shivering on the white couch for who knows how long. Heat was in short supply down there.

She traded one white couch for another when she got to Cam's loft. The striped dress that had looked so cool and crisp sixteen hours ago, hung wilted like a flower. She'd given up one of the biggest stories of the year today. His wife deserved some kind of explanation as to why this one thing was so important. Rasmussen's processing, and his and Hasting's release had gone as quickly, quietly, and smoothly as he and Rivera could have hoped. No cop liked being on the moving end of a directive from up high. But his climb back to Lieutenant had been steep. There was no way he could have afforded another fall off the promotional ladder again.

What he and Rivera had been asked to do had been one hundred percent wrong. The low level prostitutes, pimps, and drug dealers had all gone to jail or been deported. Dolores wasn't the only one to suffer the fate of deportation from the country. Two others caught up in the sweep had made their way back to Guatemala. The aides who'd helped were facing criminal conspiracy felonies.

Once the perps had started talking, he and Rivera were chomping at the bit to get the big fish. They'd issued arrest warrants for the councilman, happy to close the sting with the arrest of those with the most influence who had flouted the law.

Then they'd gotten a call to come down to West First Street, the new headquarters. The snow job took nearly an hour, but the bottom line was Hastings and Rasmussen were going to be charged with misdemeanors, processed quietly and let out on their own recognizance.

Cam had railed all the way back toward Hollywood. Rivera was silent, only speaking up once to say that the case was closed. When Jessie had called, he'd known his partner was the leak. She'd had the guts to do what he couldn't: shed light on the injustice of privilege.

And maybe they'd have been in the clear. He'd been with Jessie nearly the entire weekend. There wasn't a moment he could have leaked the story. But the flip side was that he'd been with Jessie.

When he'd told Rivera, she'd said nothing. He'd downplayed his relationship with Jessie, and Rivera had taken him at his word. She'd probably never thought the guy at KESP would assign Jessie to the case. But he had, and Jessie had never shown up when they'd let the politicians out the back door.

But he couldn't say a single word of this to her.

Cameron didn't talk. Ryan was the brother who talked. Where was that chattering fool when he needed him? Yellow pad in hand, Ryan would have been ready to go. Ready to explain why he and this woman should be together. Cam shook his head in frustration. He may be more fluent in English than Jessie, still he didn't have the words.

Joining her on the couch, he rubbed at the smudged makeup lingering under one eye. Doing what he did best, he pressed his lips to hers. But she didn't open for him.

"Not this, Cameron," she said, her hand firm against his chest.

"Then what?"

"Tell me what happened to you after KESP reported on the cockfighting sting."

He wanted to build a future with Jessie, not probe the past with a sharp stick. He gave the least information he could. "Internal Affairs investigated the breach."

Cam could see she wasn't going to let it go that easily. "What happened after that?"

"Then I walked into the mediator's office and signed the papers making our separation legal."

Jessie looked away like he'd wanted her to. These questions were coming too close for comfort. He'd taken his punishment like a man. He'd walked the beat. He'd withstood being separated from the woman he loved. He'd lifted weights to forget. The future was where he wanted to keep focus, not the past.

Too quickly, she turned back. Her dark brows knitted together. "Are you serious about us?"

"As a heart attack."

"Then you're going to have to start talking to me, Cameron. Out of bed. I can't be the only one who has to change."

"What do you want me to say?" Because he didn't talk much, every word was like a land mine in enemy territory.

She looked at him, unblinking. Pushed her hand through his hair, down his neck, across his pecs. Her manicured hand landed on Cam's heart, warming the spot where it was nearly beating out of his chest.

"What happened after the IA investigation?" Her voice was whisper soft.

He closed his eyes against the awful memories that flooded his brain. He'd worked hard to put much of this out of his mind after it happened. That had been the only way to move on.

"Rivera was investigated even though she had nothing to do with the leak." It was already hard for her being a minority and a woman in the department. Those months she was riding a desk while everyone treated the implosion like it was her fault. They figured she'd gotten too chummy with the sex workers and underworld types. But Rivera wasn't the type to cross over. She was a victim of doing her job too well. "When they got to me, I had to tell them we'd talked about the investigation. That I'd broken protocol. But Rivera's skin was saved."

"And you?"

"I had a union rep."

"Cameron. What happened to *you*?"

He turned his head, looking over his shoulder and into the past. "Lost the right to promotion for a couple years. Had to walk the beat in Hollywood on the night shift."

"You never told me."

"We weren't exactly on speaking terms."

"But—"

"But what? You told me you were done, *finito*."

"You pushed me away, Cam. You froze me out." He'd been angry. He'd had a right to be. But when he was done being angry at her, he was angry at himself for everything. "You still kept an eye on me, though," she said.

Surprised, he looked away. "You were done. I wasn't."

"How was I to know that?"

"Because…" Because she should have known he wasn't a guy to walk away from responsibility. He didn't want her to see him at his lowest. When he was working the beat, doing low level arrests, taking orders instead of giving orders.

Jessie's question, her accent heavier this late in the evening when she wasn't trying hard anymore, broke into his thoughts. "What do you want, Cam? Nothing is different from before. I'm still a reporter. Crime is big news in Los Angeles. You're still a cop with secrets. That hasn't changed."

"You're here. That's changed."

"I…Cam…"

"We were meant to be together. I've known it since you came to pick up your sister from the station. You're the most beautiful and compassionate woman I've ever known. The separation was the stupidest thing I ever did. It was easier to run away from the hard work than to stay and fight. It's my one and only regret in life. The only one, Jessie."

"But our jobs, our families always come between us."

"I think that's changed."

"I Skype with them. They asked me to wire money–"

"None of that matters. *You* matter more than the job or the family. We've both changed. Five years ago you'd have ambushed the councilmen."

"I should have. Is our city served by men who live by one standard when the rest of us live by another?"

"None of us are better for that."

"A story on KESP could have righted that wrong."

She was right about that. "Maybe." Cameron shook his head. He hated when what was right and what the LAPD did were at odds. "Sometimes the system fails." And when he was on firm footing again, maybe when he was finally promoted to a command position, he'd right those wrongs. For now he was willing to look the other way. It was a trade-off for a future when he could work on change from within.

Jessie stood, stalking to the window that overlooked the lights of the Valley. "It doesn't matter now," she said. "I'll probably be unemployed tomorrow."

"If you are, we'll tackle it together. Maybe you can jump to a better station."

"So where are we, Cam?"

"It's all about what *you* want, Jessie. Because if we walk away this time, that's it. I can't do this again. Mom may not have much tact, but she was right. I want to be married to you, have babies with you. Buy a house in the Valley. I know it's boring. But it's what I want. If you don't want the same thing, tell me now. We have to move forward one way or another. We've tiptoed around this too long."

FIFTEEN

YESENIA PACED in the small apartment. Never had her life choices been so stark. If this was only a fraction of the worry Mama had felt when making the choice to leave Mexico, Yesenia's sympathies were with her.

Throwing open the balcony doors, she let the cool, damp marine laden air rush in. On the balcony, the railing was cool under her palms. Traffic on Chandler Boulevard was as steady as her beating heart. She tried to remember a time when traffic wasn't pulsing in Los Angeles. Even on her mother's street, cars sped from Venice to Washington, trying to short-circuit lines of cars and save time. It kept the flow of cars as steady as breath.

Lifting her hands, she fished through her hair, seeking release. After she found and pulled out the rubber band, the tension on her scalp and temples eased. Even when she heard the faint squeak of the couch as Cameron rose, shuffled to the fridge, and sat back down, she didn't turn to look at him.

Plain and simple, she was afraid. Saying yes could

mean another failure. She'd failed at protecting her family, failed at keeping her career and private life separate. Two years she'd taken from Cam's career. How could he still want her after that? How could she try again after the damage she'd done?

Another story could come between them. The police were, if nothing, ripe for investigation and reporting. If they weren't doing favors for celebs or politicians, they were profiling the black and brown of the city—often with disastrous results.

On top of that, her family's new independence could turn to disaster any minute. If the cartels became too dangerous, she'd bring her mother and sister back in a heartbeat, damn the law. Could Cam live with that, knowing she'd be breaking the law a second time? Would he be okay keeping her family's shadowy undocumented life a secret?

This was it.

If she walked out this door, he'd find someone else, get married again. Another woman would have his babies. And if jealousy and regret ate her up, she'd have no one to blame but herself.

Yesenia stiffened when strong arms banded around her. Would he ask for her answer now?

But when no ultimatum came, she relaxed her body, consciously easing her shoulders down. She leaned back against the man who filled her with equal parts fear and desire.

"Cold out here," he said. A shiver coursed through her. Probably a trick of the mind. Power of suggestion. She hadn't felt a lick of cold when she'd stepped outside. And with his warm, solid frame behind her, the chill still didn't permeate.

Yesenia turned in the circle of steel-like bands of his arms until she was facing him. "I'm not sure I can be what you want, in or out of bed," she started.

The sting of rejection warred with stubbornness on Cam's face. Without words, she understood exactly what he was thinking. He needed to give her up or give her another chance.

"You are exactly what I want."

"But. There's always a 'but,' Cam."

"No buts, Jessie. I want you to…want me as much as I want you."

"You know I do," she whispered. "You know I do."

"Show me."

"I don't…" *know how*. She swallowed those last words.

His body language revealed no immediate decision about them. So she leaned forward, taking one decision away from him. She would give them one last gift. A final night together where she took the lead. That was the one thing they could do that wouldn't hurt a soul.

For the first time ever, she shook off her inhibitions. Yesenia wished them away on the wind that blew from the ocean to the desert. She wrapped her hands around his head and pulled him down for a kiss. Cam had never denied her this. And he didn't resist her now.

She molded her lips to his like she'd always wanted to, but had never had the guts to do. Sloppy, openmouthed kisses that didn't give a hoot about good girls and proper behavior. After a shout rose up from adolescent boys loitering on the sidewalk, she pulled herself away from

Cam long enough to push him back into the studio, far away from prying eyes.

With a whoosh of breath, his butt hit the couch, halting their movement. Hitching up the bottom of her dress, she straddled him, holding him steady for another one or ten of those soulful kisses. She lost count quickly.

Pulling back to take a breath, she opened her eyes. Normally the light-filled apartment would have made her feel exposed, but this time she didn't care. To hell with the cold air and the light. Crossing her arms in front of her, she lifted the dress over her head. Yesenia paused only long enough for Cam to look his fill. Then she thrust her breasts toward him, unclasping her bra. It dropped in his lap. Neither moved to retrieve it.

"Damn...Jessie...damn."

She leaned forward, brushing a nipple before his lips. Without a moment's hesitation, he caught the stiff bit of flesh. Her blood fizzed with sensation. Fighting not to let feelings overcome her, nor deter her from her singular mission, she tugged his t-shirt up until her hands could freely roam his chest. His pecs tensed, flexed, released. His tiny nipples beaded hard.

Yesenia brushed a hand against the faint stubble on his slackened jaw. In one swift motion, she pulled his shirt from him. Sliding down, she undid his belt and opened the front of his jeans. The denim was so soft from multiple washings, she worried he'd poke a hole through the weakened strands with his rock hard erection.

But the jeans were safe, and in a moment, after wiggling through the opening of his jeans and boxers, she filled her hands.

An inch at a time, she lowered herself until her knees were on the rug, the front of her thighs brushing against the cool, smooth leather of the couch. Her high school girlfriends had always said this is what men liked best, but she'd never had the guts. So she took a deep breath and pulled her husband's pulsing cock between her lips.

"Jessie…you don't…ah, damnit to hell," Cam swore. The musky scent of him made her knees go weak. Slowly, she moved her mouth up and down, using her tongue to tickle against the ridge. He bracketed her head between his big hands and thrust into her mouth, once, then twice.

The sense of power and control over his pleasure turned her on. A minute later the hard and soft feel of him disappeared from her mouth.

"I thought you wanted…" She was at a loss for the right words.

"You don't need—"

Maybe she would have to save that for another time. Too many surprises in one night might kill the man.

She was thinking there'd be another time. Shock waves rolled through her with that thought. A future with this man? That thought surprised her.

Yesenia brought herself back to the present. She wasn't ready to give up. Pulling out the condom she'd bravely bought at the drug store and tucked into her purse a week ago, she thrust the foil wrapped latex into his hands. No one had called her out or slapped her hands when she'd bought birth control. She'd taken it as a sign she was doing the right thing.

Standing, she shimmied from her underwear and got

down to the business of seducing her husband. First, she lifted one knee on the couch, then the other. Cam groaned, but held his ground. Leaning over, she grasped onto the back cushions as if hanging on for dear life. Yesenia anticipated she might need that death grip if he were nearly as aroused as she.

Mustering all the bravado she could, she whispered what she knew he wanted to hear. "Take me."

Muscles jangled with need, with nerves, with anticipation. Her desire to be filled fought with her worry that this wouldn't be enough. That trying to play the game by his rules had come too late. That….

The rip of foil came first, then two hands were gripping her shoulders. Next thing she knew, Cameron notched himself, thrust once, and she was filled to the hilt. Keeping her eyes open for once, she looked at the picture the two of them made. In an instant, she understood why men liked to look.

"Hot, right?"

She closed her eyes. Nodded.

"Open for me Jessie. Watch this."

One of his hands left her shoulder and rubbed at the tips of her breasts, his thrusts increasing the friction against her palms. The other hand moved between them, parted her.

She wanted to see. Opening her eyes, she watched his thumb seek and find her center.

"Oh, God," she moaned.

"This is all for you, Jessie."

She took charge in the only way she could think of, with more than half her brain lost to lust. "Come for me,

Cameron," Yesenia said, squeezing her inner muscles, milking her husband as best she could.

It worked.

For the first time she could ever remember, Cam faltered. His practiced and measured thrusts lost their tempo. For a single second, he stopped moving, probably trying to control himself. The friction against her from his hand increased. But she bit her lip, hard. The pain acted in counterpoint to the pleasure exploding everywhere else.

One more squeeze from Yesenia was all it took for Cameron to lose control once and for all. His movements became sloppy and jerky. A hoarse shout barked from his lungs. Still hard inside her, Cam took his time then. A single finger traced the cords of her neck, brushed each nipple, then drew pleasure from the place she craved it most. Yesenia didn't hold back. With effort, she pushed the inhibitions from her mind and allowed herself to be enveloped in bliss.

She tucked her head against his shoulder. Their breathing and hearts slowed in tandem. Growing soft, Cam pulled away and went to his bathroom. Getting wild during sex was one thing, but being naked in the stark light of the living room was another. Quickly, she pulled on her underwear, lifted her dress over her head, and smoothed it down as best she could. Digging through her purse, she located a hairbrush, pulled it out and smoothed her hair into a bun. A single fresh wipe took away her TV ready makeup.

His nudity stood in stark contrast to her fully dressed self when he came back.

In spite of his promises, even though he'd changed, and she'd matured, she still wasn't sure. She needed time.

"How long?" she asked.

"Jessie, don't—"

She clutched her bag to her side, ready to walk out the door. "Give me your deadline."

"Why do it this way?"

"I need time."

"Time apart?"

"Time to think."

"What do you need to know that you don't yet?"

She sighed, exhausted. Was it too much to want to decide the rest of her life when she was well rested, clear headed? Making the decision to marry was easy the first time. Given how it had turned out, far too easy. She didn't want to go into this blind the second time around. It would hurt too much if she made the same mistakes again. Love wasn't enough.

Cam hated being pushed. But if he wanted to throw around ultimatums, then she needed something concrete.

"How long?" she asked for the last time.

A pained look accompanied his next words. But he spoke them nevertheless. "One month, Jessie."

SIXTEEN

TWENTY-SEVEN DAYS LATER.

Best thing about his building was that it had a gym. Not some tiny closet holding a sole elliptical pretending to be a gym, but an honest-to-goodness weight room with Nautilus machines, treadmills, and a TV.

He lay back against the bench, pushing two hundred fifty pound weights into ten chest presses. Then twenty. The twinge in his stomach wasn't from the three hundred crunches, but from anxiety no amount of exercise could push away.

One hundred squats later, he gave himself a break. He wasn't the person who'd sent Dolores and Reina to Mexico. But he'd been the unwitting catalyst. For that, a hundred push-ups was penance. Not sufficient punishment, but what he could do to shake the guilt today and all the days so far he hadn't seen Jessie? Ten miles on the treadmill, and he'd half convinced himself his wife would come back to him.

How stupid was he to give her a month? He'd have waited years. He'd already waited two.

Three days remained. Rivera and Ryan had both warned him. Under no circumstances was he to go to Jessie and grovel. He'd laid down the gauntlet. If there was truly any chance of them coming together, she'd have to want it as much as he. She had to be as invested in their future.

Intellectually, he knew that. But his heart was beating out of his chest with either the exertion from exercise or worry that he'd played his last card and was still going to lose to the house.

Checking the time on his heart rate monitor, Cam quickly wiped down the equipment and ran upstairs. He didn't take elevators much himself anymore. Years ago, Jessie had gotten him into the stair habit and he'd never quit.

It was time to see his wife. He didn't have time for a shower, so he stood to watch the ten o'clock news, sweat cooling on his skin. If it weren't for Jessie, he'd never have made it through a local newscast. The nightly coverage never changed from murder and mayhem. Didn't matter which station he watched.

Tonight a homicide investigation topped her newscast. But with over two hundred fifty a year in L.A., that wasn't news. Jessie stood next to Yolanda Salcedo, legs on display, while their seriously dour and three piece suited co-anchor Hector Garcia talked about crime and the effect it had on the residents of L.A.'s so called "Homicide Alley."

Next up, Jessie threw it to a reporter interviewing

teenagers on immigration reform. He didn't need total fluency to understand the weather—cold on the coast, hot in the desert—same as it was every day. Or the traffic—bad.

He risked a five minute shower and was back after the last commercial for the close. Though he personally hated Jessie's exploitation, he enjoyed watching her walk off set with her co-anchor and the geriatric Garcia. Tonight his wife was encased in a tight black skirt that ended just at her knees. He may not be able to touch her, but the image of her swaying butt should at least make for a fulfilling night of fantasies.

But Jessie didn't stride off the set tonight. The camera zoomed in on her face as she spoke earnestly.

"Quiero agradecer a todos aquí en KESP por todo su apoyo durante mis diez años aquí. Aunque estoy triste por dejar..." He couldn't keep up with her Spanish. Leaving. To go where?

He picked up his phone then put it down uselessly. Obviously he couldn't call her while she was on the air. For the next five minutes he paced the tiny apartment. When the credits were done, he dialed Jessie.

It rang.

No answer.

He didn't leave a message.

Pent up energy nearly choked the life out of him. Maybe he'd go for a run around North Hollywood Park. Resolved to running, he changed into a second pair of sweats, got his keys and wallet.

He was nearly out the door when he remembered. All parks closed at dusk. He'd swept hundreds of them in his day. Fuck it. If he encountered any cops, he'd badge his way out of trouble. Added his shield to his bulging pocket.

Cam picked up his phone one last time, punching in Jessie's number.

"Hello," she answered, cool as a cucumber.

"You're leaving KESP?"

Her sigh was long. "I'm at Mama's house."

Summoned, finally, he ran down to his car. Finding the right button on the fob, he got the door open and threw himself into the car, slamming the door. He resisted the urge to speed to South L.A. He needed to arrive in one piece.

The neighborhood was both eerily quiet and noisy all at the same time. There wasn't a lick of activity on her street as the hour approached midnight. But high in the sky helicopters, night suns blazing, patrolled the neighborhoods, their rotors a distant *whomp-whomp* in the air.

Locking the car, he strode up the walk. Jessie stood behind the security door. Light from the house silhouetted her.

"What are you doing here?" he asked.

"I moved in," she said.

"To your mother's house?"

"Our house." She twisted the lock and pushed open the door, stepping back. "Mama and Dori don't look like they're leaving Mexico."

Cam followed her in. He was taken aback. Original hardwood gleamed. The rooms were painted in muted colors. Gone was the pink Reina had loved so much. The butt ugly projection TV and squishy leather sofas had been replaced with Jessie's tasteful furniture.

"I didn't want to pay rent and a mortgage too. I'd been so depressed about losing out on my own condo. But I woke up a couple of weeks ago and realized I already owned a home of my own."

He wanted to ask if she felt safe in South Los Angeles but thought better of it. If the LAPD couldn't protect her, then his job wasn't worth the badge he carried in his pocket.

"What about KESP?" The thing that had come between again and again.

"I had it out with Ernesto," she started. "During the ten years I've worked there, the station went from community news to tabloid press. KESP wasn't TMZ, but it was starting to feel that way."

He sat on a kitchen stool while she poured two glasses of white wine. Cold chardonnay wasn't his favorite, but he knew better than to protest. He stayed put and sipped at the cool liquid on the dining room side of the pass. She remained in the kitchen, not drinking, but twirling the wine stem between her fingers.

"Ernesto suggested I talk to a friend of his. It was more than a suggestion. The writing was on the wall after I walked away from the Hastings story. I updated my reel. He did me a good turn. His friend turned out to be an executive at Univision."

Pride expanded in his chest. Had his Jessie finally reached her dream? "So?"

Her smile lit up the dimmed rooms. "I start in three weeks," she said. "I'll be working for Univision *Investiga*—their investigative news division."

Happiness spread through his limbs. He made his way around the arch to the kitchen, picking her up in a bear hug.

"Cam?" she asked in surprise.

"So proud of you." She'd finally be doing what she'd trained for all these years. Less exploitation and sensationalism. More hard news.

As he loosened his arms, she slid down his body, jolting him to awareness. Gently, but firmly, he pushed her away. He couldn't let pride get mixed with lust.

"Three days..." he started.

"I was going to call you tomorrow morning, Cam," she said, her face a picture of seriousness.

"What were you going to say?"

"Move in with me?"

Disappointment sucked out the buoyancy of pride and love that had filled him. "I want more than a roommate, Jessie."

She shook her head slowly. "Don't you want to try again? See if it works?"

He'd had no intention of doing this here, or doing this tonight, and not in LAPD issue sweats. But he grabbed her hand and went down on one knee before her. He closed his eyes, gathering all the resolve he'd need to walk away if she said "no."

"*Cásate conmigo.* Marry me, Yesenia."

Her face pinched in misunderstanding. "You're learning Spanish? Cam—"

He shook his head, silencing her. "I'm not finished. *Te quiero.* I love you. I want to be with you from right this moment until the day I die. I don't care where we live, or where you work. We'll figure all of it out. I want us to figure it out together.

"Yesenia Guadalupe Morales, you are the first and

only woman I've ever loved." Cam sucked much needed air and courage into his lungs. *"Cásate conmigo...de nuevo."*

She dropped her lids. When she opened her eyes, he knew he'd won. She nodded before she spoke. *"Sí."*

Wrapping her in another hug, in her ear he whispered the words he'd said on their wedding day all those years before. "Once mine, always mine."

"Once yours, always yours," she whispered back.

EPILOGUE

"WHAT ARE YOU DOING IN HERE?" Yesenia asked, knocking on open door, but not entering the room.

They'd turned Dolores' old bedroom into a study. Cam liked her at home on the nights he wasn't working. So they'd pulled up the carpet and installed a large desk. When she was developing a story, she made the phone calls and connections required to put on good television news.

Other nights, he was there by himself. Acknowledging the confidential nature of his investigations, she gave him space to do what he needed. They'd even agreed on a knock first policy.

Cam started, his concentration on the screen in front of him broken. "Sorry," she said.

"Don't be. You may as well come in." Cam's tone was resigned.

Dread fogged her brain. Everything had been going so well. They'd slipped back into married life without so much as a hiccough.

"Jessie, don't look like that. Just come here."

Slowly, she made her way into the room. She let Cam pull her on to his lap. Things were starting to get a little better. Yesenia wiggled her bottom. Certain things certainly felt a little better. "What do you have in mind?"

"Not that."

"Not that? I think your body says a little different."

Cam shifted her toward his knees. Despite her usual self censoring, she looked at the papers on his desk. They looked like loose pages from a Spanish language workbook. Mirrors of what she'd studied in ESL classes.

"You're studying Spanish? I don't need you to speak my language," she said. It was true. She'd finally gotten off her high horse about everyone in the L.A. basin learning Spanish.

"It's not just for you. I have something else to tell you."

Fear of their future returned. "What?" He flipped open the laptop. The screen flickered, then came into focus. "You're on a airline website? Why?"

"We'd talked about what do with our vacation time this year."

Yesenia's "Sure," was full of hesitation. They'd talked about trying for a baby during a week in Hawaii or Jamaica. She hoped he hadn't changed his mind about that.

"I have a few minutes to click 'buy,' but I want your okay," he said.

"Where do you think we should go?"

"Mexico City," he said. "I talked to Reina and Dolores and they'd love for us to visit."

"Seriously?" Yesenia's eyes filled blurring the letters

and numbers on the screen. "You'd spend your vacation with my family?"

"You need to see for yourself that they're okay," Cam said.

"What about the baby making?"

"We'll stay in a hotel for the nights. I can get us a suite at this place." He flicked to another window and a picture of a hotel room appeared complete with hot tub, and outdoor fire pit.

"*Sí.*" She cleared her throat. "Yes."

"Go. I can't do this with you distracting me," he said lifting her from his lap.

"I'll get ready for bed. I'll be waiting."

"Don't worry, babe. I'll be there as soon as I can click 'buy' and type in our credit card number."

Yesenia put her hands to her heart, filled to nearly bursting with love. "Seriously, Cam. Thank you."

"Anything for you, babe. Always remember that." Cam turned back to the screen.

She made her way to their newly painted bedroom. Maybe they could get a head start on the baby making.

The End

Thanks so much for reading **Shaken**. Impasse was the first book in the Hollywood Studs Series. It was a stand-alone and I never anticipated that one day it would be five books. But I fell head over heels for Ryan and his cantankerous mom and wanted to know more about them. Cameron grunted through their meal and I had to write his story.

After that I wanted to know more about Nick's elusive brother and sister. *Stirred* is Zoe Andreis' story. A family health scare brings her back from Europe. She literally falls for the first guy she meets: bus driver Max Kiss. Never was a more swoon worthy hero born. Bus drivers get big, strong arms wrestling that huge steering wheel every day…read on for *Stirred*.

"A sweet quirky love story with an interesting cast of characters. A fun read." —*Kim P.*

Zoe

I got the three A.M. call no one ever wants. After I fumbled and dropped the phone, I finally heard the news I'd always dreaded. My father was in the hospital and no one knew what was wrong with him. I was in Europe six thousand miles away from Los Angeles.

I hopped one plane, then another. Then I was on a city bus to the hospital because I was stuck in L.A. without a car, which was like being in a river without a boat *and* without a paddle. The city wasn't looking like it was going to be so lonely once I got the bus driver Max's number, though.

Max

Zoe actually asked me to let her know which stop was hers. None of my riders talked to me unless it was go get out of paying the fare. This one did. She was tall, pretty, and looked upset. So I gave her my number. Never expected her to call. But she did and I brought her home and then...I helped her feel better.

But her father got better and she wasn't planning to stay. She was ready to go off on her next adventure when all I wanted was for her to stay in Los Angeles—for me. I hugged her, let her get on a plane...and now all I have to do convince her to come back to me. For a woman with wanderlust, that's not going to be easy.

ABOUT THE AUTHOR

I write crazy, beautiful love stories because I believe story-telling is magic. I love complicated heroines with secrets, strong heroes who fall hard, and a long winding road to happily ever after. When I'm not writing, I love to travel to witness the diverse tapestry of humanity, photograph the beauty of the world, visit museums, and watch live theater. I live in West Hollywood, California ten miles from the nearest airport.

♥

I'm the host of Fifty First Dates the Podcast. I haven't found my own happily ever after, but I'm not done look-ing. Join me as I try to find my Mr. Right or maybe Mr.

Right Now in Southern California. #50firstdates #joliemoore #crazybeautifullove